MOUNTAIN COUSINS

GERALDINE GARDNER GIRARD

Author's Tranquility Press
MARIETTA, GEORGIA

Geraldine Gardner Girard/Author's Tranquility Press
2706 Station Club Drive SW
Marietta, GA 30060
www.authorstranquilitypress.com

Publisher's Note: This is a work of fiction. Names, characters, places, and incidents are a product of the author's imagination. Locales and public names are sometimes used for atmospheric purposes. Any resemblance to actual people, living or dead, or to businesses, companies, events, institutions, or locales is completely coincidental.

Ordering Information:
Quantity sales. Special discounts are available on quantity purchases by corporations, associations, and others. For details, contact the "Special Sales Department" at the address above.

Mountain Cousins/Geraldine Gardner Girard
Hardback: 978-1-959197-21-8
Paperback: 978-1-959197-22-5
eBook: 978-1-959197-23-2

THIS BOOK IS DEDICATED TO:

M. Jason Girard

Richard Dillingham

Susan Bell

Steve Casper

(Owner – PC Solutions)

Cover Photo: Toe River, Burnsville, NC

By Gera Girard

CONTENTS

CHAPTER 1
THE FIRE

The lights peeked over the blue green North Carolina Mountains deep in the heart of the Blue Ridge. The sun shot its arrows of light across the peaks, turning the shadows around the ridges dark purple. The sky had already changed to its soft baby blue as a plume of black smoke invaded this glowing scene. It drifted upward through the tall dark green pines and hovered in the morning air as the smell of wood smoke spread across the valley.

Three small children lay comfortably curled up in one large feather bed in a small log cabin in that valley. On this late summer morning in 1914, the heat had not yet blanketed the mountains. The heat never got as bad as it did in the foothills even in late summer. Mornings were light and crisp and the light cotton quilt that covered the children invited a little more time spent under its protection.

The first born child, eleven-year-old Lila Ann, slept facing the door on the outside with six-year-old Anna Jane, the middle child, curled up right next to two-year-old Jimmy, the youngest. Before Anna Jane's bright blue eyes opened every morning she liked to stretch her legs. Only this morning one small foot ended up in the middle of Lila Ann's back. This set off a chain reaction.

"Anna Jane," Lila Ann growled, "Move over and get your foot out of my back!" Lila Ann gave Anna Jane a shove, disturbing Jimmy beside her. Jimmy let out a howl that set their Daddy's coon dogs to baying, ready to tree the coon that woke them up. All this commotion brought both girls up in bed, Lila Ann toppling to the floor!

"Ouch!" Lila Ann hollered, stretching her long legs out in front of her, she looked back up to the warm bed, her strawberry-colored braids falling across her back. Her two siblings smiled down at her from under the cotton quilt. "I sorry," said Jimmy. Anna Jane just giggled as she reached her hand down to her sister.

"I'm okay." Lila Ann said as she smacked gently at Anna Jane's hand and grabbed the edge of the bed to pull herself up. Lila Ann, tall for her age, stood up slowly so she wouldn't lose her balance. As she stood, she heard her parents' voices drift in from the back porch.

The little log house where all the children were born consisted of two rooms, a kitchen and a living room. The living room doubled as the bedroom for the entire family. The kitchen had its own entrance from the back porch. This room had been added later after the main cabin had been built. It had a new cast iron wood-burning cook stove bought with money Charles had saved from selling animal skins he hunted in the fall and winter and ordered from a Sears, Roebuck and Company of Minnesota catalog.

Her parents stood close together on the porch, deep in quiet conversation. Charles Ireland was a large man with a short, curly beard. He was dressed in his usual attire of bib top overalls with a plaid shirt, the sleeves rolled up to expose the rippling muscles in his arms. He had been up for hours and had already finished his morning chores. Charles made a living as a sharecropper. This meant he didn't own the land he farmed it belonged to Zeb Cox but shared the crop he brought in with Zeb. The land he farmed bordered the farm that belonged to the children's aunt and uncle. Charles had a hot cup of coffee in his hands and he blew on it as he and, Lockie, Lila Ann's mother talked.

Lockie had strawberry-colored hair too, coming from the Scotch Irish on her father's side of the family. A tall woman at 5' 8" in her stocking feet, Lockie towered over most of the women in her community. She was known for her singing at community gatherings, much as her mother had, she sung old songs that originated in Scotland and England.

The couple had been discussing what Lockie would fix for breakfast when the smell of burning wood bad enough to sting the eyes had brought their attention to the back porch. "Lockie look here! I told you I smelled smoke that was more than someone's chimney fire!"

Charles aimed the steaming cup of coffee in the direction of the source of the smoke outside, "I knew Zeb Cox would find someone to do his dirty work for him when I turned him down!"

A cabin across the valley from the Ireland's was well engulfed in flames that blazed from every window, had a dark plume of smoke beginning to drift horizontally across the valley. As Charles and Lockie watched, several riders arrived along with a wagon carrying tools and buckets. The men on horseback scrambled around, placing their horses well away from the flames, and grabbed buckets off of their wagon then ran to the nearby creek to carry water.

"It's too late to save that cabin," Charles commented as he finally sipped his coffee. "I guess I'd better go help them keep it from catching the trees and coming over here on us."

The mention of fire brought Lila Ann out of the house and onto the back porch where she could see the action below. As Lila Ann scurried outside, both of the other children jumped up on the bed so they too could see the action through the window. Jimmy, not tall enough to really see anything, started to whine, "I can't see, I can't see."

"Come on, Jimmy,". Anna Jane said grabbing his hand and dragging him out of the bed with her, "We can see from the back porch."

Charles turned, as all three of his children in their bedclothes appeared hanging over the railing of the back porch. He stooped down to pick up his small son, who still couldn't see much because his head barely reached the top of the porch railing. "Fire, Daddy, fire." Jimmy pointed his tiny finger toward the clearing below.

"Yes, son and I need to go down there to help them get that fire put out," Charles said as he walked toward Lockie and handed Jimmy over into her arms. As Charles headed down through the yard, Lockie turned to holler at him, "Charles, please do be careful, you hear?"

Lockie turned back to the girls as they hung on the railing watching their father appear down at the clearing where the other men were working feverishly to put out the flames, "Girls, go get dressed. I'll need some help with breakfast. Your Pappy will be hungry when he gets back. He may bring people back with him that will need feeding as well."

The girls turned around to enter the back door and scoop up their clothes they left at the end of the bed. Lockie carried Jimmy on her hip as she entered the door that led to the kitchen from the back porch. She called over her shoulder, "Hurry up and get dressed, Lila Ann and come help me with breakfast."

Lila Ann grumbled as she slid into her dress, "I sure am glad its summer and I don't have to worry about wearing those stiff old shoes with all them buttons."

"Help!" cried Anna Jane from underneath her dress, "I can't find the head hole!"

"Oh, Anna Jane, no one helped me get my clothes on when I was your age," Lila Ann said as she walked over to give Anna Jane's dress a yank. "Now, come on, I'm getting hungry."

As the girls walked onto the back porch and started to enter the kitchen door, the cabin in the clearing below collapsed as the fire consumed it. Lockie, hearing the swish of the house collapsing, stepped back out onto the porch with Jimmy still on her hip. Jimmy saw his Pappy jumping back from the flying embers that blew out from the collapsing building.

"Look, Mommy, there's Pappy!" Jimmy exclaimed. Lockie held Jimmy close running her fingers through his soft brown curls. "Yes, Jimmy, that's your Pappy down there." With the cabin gone Lockie thought soon the fire would be out and Charles would return home. She saw some men pouring water down around the surrounding trees close to the cabin area. Soon the small wooden building would be nothing but a pile of smoking ashes. The men began collecting the buckets and tools and talking. Charles turned to acknowledge his audience up at his own cabin using his bandana to wave at them across the trees. The Ireland cabin was higher up on the mountain than the McCall cabin, and Charles looked very small to his family.

"Hey, Pappy!" both girls said as they jumped up and down and waved back, "Mommy," Lila Ann turned to her mother, "the fire is out and Pappy is a hero!"

Lockie frowned as she placed Jimmy next to Anna Jane on the stoop and said, "Yes, well, I guess. Come on in with me now, Lila Ann, and let's get breakfast started. Your hero Pappy will be very hungry when he gets to the house. Anna Jane, take Jimmy in and help get him dressed. Then you both can go out back and play until breakfast is ready. And don't either one of you go out of this yard!"

"Yes, Mommy," Anna Jane replied as she took her little brother's hand, "Let's get you dressed, Jimmy, and then we '11 go play."

Lockie fried fatback in the large black cast iron frying pan and Anna Jane took Jimmy out under the shade tree to play. Lila Ann called this area a playhouse. The children's only toys were homemade ones; playthings made out of sticks and stones and bits of broken dishes, old tools and scraps of material from Lockie's quilt making. Charles had already entered the yard as the children sat down on the soft tan dirt to play.

"Pappy," Jimmy said as he jumped up from the ground to greet his father.

Charles reached down and with one hand pulled Jimmy up on his shoulder. Anna Jane was close behind him as she said, "Pappy, you are a hero! You put out the fire!"

The smell of hot biscuits and fatback gravy drifted out the kitchen door. Lila Ann had just started setting the table with a round white cake of fresh creamy butter. Lila Ann had a bit of pride in the making of the butter yesterday by shaking the cream she had skimmed off of the fresh milk into a large canning jar. Her favorite Granny had showed her how to do this the winter that Jimmy had been born when she had come to stay with them for a while and help Lockie. Lila Ann thought this process almost magic the way the clumps of cream would form butter when you shook the jar.

"My goodness, I'm hungry!" exclaimed Charles as he entered the kitchen bending low so Jimmy's head wouldn't hit the doorsill. "Look at that fresh butter! Did you make that, Lila Ann?"

"Yes, Pappy," Lila Ann said with a twinkle in her eye, "Just like Granny Mae showed me with that pretty wooden butter form Grandpa carved for her. See, it has a little flower on top."

Charles handed Jimmy over to Lockie so he could get cleaned up for breakfast. "That sure going to taste good on those hot biscuits your Mommy has made."

Charles stepped over to a small pump that emptied into the sink and began pumping water. Lockie already had a small metal dishpan full of water with soap and a towel close by to wash Jimmy's face and hands. Jimmy squirmed as Lockie washed his face. She had parked Jimmy on the top of the counter because it was getting hard to hold him.

She had a larger stomach now because she carried a fourth child that would be born in two months.

"I'm glad the McCall's got moved out last week," Lockie commented as she sat Jimmy in his wooden high chair. "Bess McCall was a good neighbor and friend and I will miss her. It was nice having someone close after I had Jimmy and Granny went home."

"Lockie, don't worry none. Your sister insists we come up there and stay when it is time for the new babe." Charles had already sat down after he helped the girls get the rest of the table set. He had poured milk for the children and more coffee for himself and Lockie. He broke biscuits for the girls and poured thick white gravy over the biscuits. He then placed the fatback curls of pork meat onto his plate. Lockie had also made some applesauce. It sat warming on the stove. The apple trees in the front yard had been full of juicy green cooking apples this year. Lockie had been busy canning them the week before.

"What did Zeb have to say about the fire?" Lockie asked as she sat down to eat.

"Everyone got kind of silent when I got over there," Charles began, "Zeb Cox thanked me for helping but everyone else acted kind of strange."

"Pappy, you are a hero!" Anna Jane exclaimed again.

Charles tousled Anna Jane's curly brown hair, "Sure, I am, bright eyes,"

Charles turned to give Lockie a look. They both knew this conversation would have to continue later after the children went to bed. While Lockie cleaned the breakfast dishes Charles stepped out on the back porch with his coffee to survey the now smoking pile of ashes down below the side of the mountain. Lockie joined him, circling her arms around his waist.

Lila Ann appeared at the back door, "Mommy, can we go to Uncle Fate's today? I can't wait to tell Joe Heniy all about the fire! He always tells me stories about his grandfather, the Frenchman, and stories about that ghost he's seen up in the holler. Now, I have something to tell him.

Charles and Lockie looked at each other. "Well, I guess we do need to go over to Fate's," Charles said, "I need to talk to him about this whole matter that happened this morning."

Turning to Lila Ann, Lockie said, "Help me get your brother and sister ready. I can pack some food to take for the dinner meal. Hurry now!"

"Yeah, and I have an axe head Fate said he'd sharpen for me," Charles replied as he headed for his tool shed. Charles, also concerned about what had happened at the fire that morning, wanted to discuss it with his brother-in-law. If there was going to be trouble, he would need Fate's help for sure.

CHAPTER 2
THE VISIT

As Lockie prepared food to take to her sister's place. Lila Ann helped Anna Jane and Jimmy put on clean clothes. It had been over a week since she had visited her two cousins. She always enjoyed spending time with them, thirteen-year-old Joe Henry and nine-year-old Nathan Laboree. The Laboree family owned 200 acres of land that bordered the Tennessee state line. Lockie's older sister, Ora had married Lafayette (Fate) Laboree when Lockie was just a little girl. Ora, ten years older than Lockie, lived in a big two-story white house built by Fate's father not far from the little Baptist Church and schoolhouse that their five children and the Ireland's three children attended.

"Are we ready? I found that axe head," Charles said as he grabbed a crumb of biscuit from the counter while Lockie worked preparing food to take to her sister's.

"Yes," Lockie said, "round up the young'uns and we'll head down the road. You know, I'm sure glad you cut that path through the laurel thicket. It won't take us half the time to walk to Fate's now."

Charles put his arm around Lockie, kissed her forehead and gently patted her round stomach. "Are you sure I shouldn't put you in the sled and me and the young'uns pull you?" Charles said with a little chuckle.

"Oh, Charles, you silly goose," Lockie said, "We need to get moving so we can get there before dinner time. I can manage walking just fine, thank you!"

Charles grabbed the metal bucket that once contained lard and now made an excellent food bucket and out the door the couple headed. Greeting the children in the front yard, the little family headed down the path and through the laurel thicket to the Laboree home.

Two miles away, Ora Laboree worked in her front yard finishing up a chore that she had started at the crack of dawn, washing clothes. The water had been boiling since before daybreak in a large black kettle.

"Rose, is there anymore room on that line over there beyond the smoke house?" Ora asked.

"No, Mamma, but I can hang some things on the picket fence," seventeen-year-old Rose answered. Rose, the only girl of the Laboree's children had been living at the Wilson's home near Asheville for the past three years so she could attend high school. Rose planned to get married in the fall to a young man who worked for a small college near Asheville.

Joe Henry came running through the yard with a smaller freckled faced shadow behind him. "Mamma, I heard about a fire over near Uncle Charles's this morning!"

"Yeah, we overheard some of the men at Cox's store that rode up on horses as they talked about that house Tom McCall used to live in," Nathan echoed from behind his brother.

Nathan stood about to the shoulders of his brother, Joe Henry. He had his mother's red hair. Joe Henry had dark hair like his father and his grandfather's dark twinkling eyes.

"Mamma, I bet Uncle Charles and Aunt Lockie come over today," Joe Henry noted.

"Yes, I suspect they will. It has been over a week since Lockie's family has come calling. It has been a busy time with canning and all. And she is busy getting ready for that new baby too. I know they would have seen that fire from the old cabin. Charles probably helped put that fire out," Ora said, "Come on, Rose, help me start dinner. Nathan, go into the smoke house and find me that large ham. I'll slice some of that meat for dinner and Joe Henry, go find your Pa and tell him we'll be having company."

"Yes, Mamma, but Pa heard about the fire at the store so I reckon he'll figure as much too."

"I sure will," Fate said as he rode up into the yard on his wagon, "Come here, Joe Henry, and unhitch these mules." Fate Laboree, a tall dark man with a mustache that twilled up at either end, looked a lot like his father, the Frenchman. Fate loved music and played the fiddle at the local corn shucking and other community get togethers. His father had made music too. He had come to the mountains with an organ grinder and a trained monkey. He had won them in a card game in New Orleans. The monkey had become part of his family and when it died they buried it in the family cemetery on top of the mountain.

As Joe Henry and Nathan set off to do the tasks their parents had given them another son who looked much like his father rode up on a horse into the yard. Eighteen-year-old William Laboree, the oldest of the Laboree children, called Willie by most courted the neighbor's daughter. "Papa, did you hear about the fire?" Willie said as he dismounted his horse.

"Yes, the boys and I heard about the fire at Cox's store when Zeb and some of the others rode up with the news."

Down the road the Ireland family made their way toward the Laboree house. Unless you had a horse or mules and a wagon the feet did most of the traveling in the mountains. The narrow mountain roads made it rough on any traveler. Charles had to take a slower stride to allow his family to keep up with him and he walked at a leisurely pace. The sun and the children played hide and seek along the road, in and out of the laurel thicket. The leaves in the trees gently rustled and the smell of honeysuckle drifted through the air.

"Even though I'm on my feet most of the day, this walking makes me feel better," Lockie said.

"If you'd like to stop and rest a while we can," Charles said.

"No, I'm fine."

Suddenly the sound of giggling floated around the young couple. Charles stopped and turned to check and see where the children played. "You three come out here from the woods. Don't get into that laurel thicket too far. You'll get tangled up and lost in there!"

Lila Ann burst from behind a bush and Anna Jane not far behind with little Jimmy in tow. "I told you that she's in there with her axe, ready to chop off your heads!"

"Pappy, Lila Ann is scaring me and Jimmy when we're in those woods! She says that woman Joe Henry told us about that killed her husband and chopped him up is in the woods!" Anna Jane cried.

"Here now, Lila Ann, you stop scaring your sister and brother like that. That woman got hung in Morganton eighty years ago and she's buried down there some where," Charles replied.

"Charles Ireland, you talk about that with those young'uns and they'll have nightmares tonight!" Lockie said as she grabbed her husband's arm to give it a little shake.

"Oh, Lockie, young'uns love haint stories. I don't know why but I sure enjoyed them when I was a boy. Besides, they first heard about our Frankie from Joe Henry. It makes the story even better when it comes from a true story." Charles said as he patted Lockie's hand.

"Well, I don't care if Frankie killed her husband or not, I just don't want to be up with our young'uns all night. I need my sleep, I don't know about you!"

"We're here!" Lila Ann said as she ran past her parents to enter the clearing first. As she did she sent chickens clucking and scurrying everywhere. With all the commotion Joe Henry and Nathan came bounding out of the house and onto the front porch to greet their cousins. Lila Ann climbed up the porch steps so she would be the first to share the exciting story of the morning.

"I woke up this morning to the smell of smoke and a fire that raged down the hill below us at the Tom McCall cabin! I watched that cabin burn to the ground!" Lila Ann said breathlessly.

Anna Jane followed behind Lila Ann pulling Jimmy up the steps with her, "And Pappy is a hero cause he helped to put the fire out!"

The screen door squeaked as Ora stepped outside holding her youngest son, Jesse. Three-year-old Jesse looked like his brother, Nathan, with curly red hair. "Fate and the boys were at Cox's store this morning when Zeb and some of his men returned from the McCall cabin. I told Joe Henry I bet Charles would help put that fire out. The McCalls moved out last week, didn't they? I sure hope they did, anyway. I saw Bess McCall at church a couple of weeks ago and she said that they were moving."

"Yes, they were gone about last Wednesday and it sure is a good thing. Bess came over to the house last week and said they were thinking of staying another month but they had to go help tend to her mother over in Erwin cause she fell and broke her hip," Lockie said as Charles helped her up the steps.

"I'm fixing dinner. You plan to stay, don't you?"

"I brought some biscuits and some of my new applesauce," Lockie said handing Ora the bucket. "I think those apples are the best crop I've had since Lila Ann was born."

"Good, come in and sit and rest. I know carrying that extra little load is tiring. Your feet look a might swelled. Come on in and we'll prop them up," Ora said gently taking her sister by the arm as she placed Jesse down next to his cousin, Jimmy.

"Lila Ann, you and Anna Jane watch those little boys. Take them out in the yard to play and don't let Jimmy chase those chickens. That old rooster will flog him," Lockie said as she disappeared into the house with Ora.

Charles had met Fate coming around the side of the house, "I brought this axe head you said I could sharpen."

"Sure, come out to my workshop in the barn and we'll fix it up for you," Fate said as he studied Charles's face, "Did Zeb mention anything to you about how the cabin caught fire? I mean, he knows you didn't do it?"

"I suppose. He never said a word and he sure wouldn't look me in the eye. A man acts like that means only one thing, dishonesty. I tell you, Fate, I don't trust that man."

"Reckon who he got to set that fire?" Fate speculated.

"I don't know but someone got his price. One of Zeb's hired men that helped put out the fire asked me if I would be doing the sharecropping on the land that the McCalls use to work now that the cabin is gone and no one will be living there to work that land. I thought to myself, where in the world did he get that idea?"

While the men worked in the barn and the women busied themselves in the kitchen preparing dinner, the children got together in the backyard to talk and play. Whenever the cousins got together, Joe Henry usually did most of the talking. A born storyteller, Joe Henry always had tales of his Grandfather who came from France at age fifteen and traveled across the states to settle in the mountains and marry a farmer's daughter or the ghost story of the young mountain girl who killed her husband

and got hung for it in the 1830s. Today Lila Ann had everyone's attention, and she enjoyed every minute of it.

"You could smell the smoke. It got so strong it made my eyes water!" she exclaimed as she pointed to both of her eyes. Lila Ann turned to each child looking into their eyes and continued, "And as we got out to the back porch, the cabin below made this loud crash! The roof caved in and the flames shot up real high!" Lila Ann stretched on her toes imitating the flames.

Nathan's eyes got as big as saucers and Joe Henry's mouth opened as their eyes followed her wiggling fingers up into the air. When Lila Ann finished, she sat down on a hollow log and smiled.

"Gosh!" Nathan exclaimed, "I have never seen a fire that big!"

"Yeah, those men were talking about it at the store. Remember, Nathan?" Nathan nodded yes as Joe Henry continued, "I think they were talking about how it started, but when we came up they hushed. Anyway, I bet it was no accident. We haven't had a storm in over a week."

The smell of cured ham, warm biscuits and hot applesauce drifted toward the little group as Rose walked up to announce the dinner meal was ready. "You young'uns go get washed up on the back porch. Lila Ann, how are you sweetie? Come help me get Jesse and Jimmy cleaned up, won't you?"

"Yes 'um," Lila Ann thought Rose was the most beautiful girl in the valley with her long dark hair and blue eyes. Whenever she and Anna Jane played Lila Ann would always pretend that she was Rose. And whenever Lila Ann's teacher loaned her fairy tale books she would read them to her Mommy and Pappy in the evening. And in her mind she pictured Rose as a beautiful princess. Taking her little brother's hand she followed behind Rose and Jesse trying to imitate the graceful way that Rose walked through the yard.

CHAPTER 3
SCHOOLDAYS

The warm evenings began to tum cooler and the harvest time came to an end. It also came time for the children in the community to prepare to head out each morning for the six-month free school in the little mountain community. All of the children in the mountain cove near the Laboree farm attended a little one-room school that doubled as the Baptist Church and community building.

Besides the path that Charles had cut through the laurel thicket to make it easier for his children to walk to school, he had also built two new log footbridges across the creek so they would have a safer trip to school. He had even worked on the main road trimming trees and filling ruts in the road as the state often expected the farmers to help take care of the mountain roads so the bad weather didn't make them impassible. The Laboree farm was along the way so Lila Ann always stopped by on her way to school. Many times if the weather got bad, Joe Henry and Nathan would come to the Ireland place and walk Lila Ann to school because the school never closed because of bad weather.

"Lila Ann, will I be able to write my name today?" questioned Anna Jane as the girls began their journey to school. This would be Anna Jane's first day of school.

"Oh, Anna Jane, it may take you a while before you can. You have to learn to make the letters first."

"Are them the things you scratched in the dirt with a stick the other day?"

"Yes, Mr. Wills will show you on the blackboard with chalk. I really like Mr. Wills. He taught me how to read," Lila Ann carried the food bucket with their applesauce biscuits in it. Lockie had also made eggs with the biscuits that morning and she always made extra biscuits for the school lunch and for Charles to have. Charles always came looking mid-morning before time for her to prepare his lunch.

Joe Henry always waited for Lila Ann when she walked to school. Today he had two little cousins to wait on as they entered the clearing at the Laboree farm. The boys had been up for hours and had finished their chores, which included getting the cows in from the high pasture on top of the mountain, milking them and turning them back out. Joe Henry had also helped Willie and his father fix a wheel on the wagon that had gotten broken the day before. Nathan had gathered the eggs for his mother that morning before they had breakfast. Nathan came around the corner of the house tossing a brand new baseball.

"Wow!" Lila Ann exclaimed, "Where did you get that, Nathan?"

"I got it from money I earned working some for Zeb Cox at his store delivering things to his customers. I ordered it from a mail order catalog."

Joe Henry and Nathan tossed the ball back and forth as they followed the girls down the road toward school. Joe Henry said, "We should be able to have a fine game of baseball at recess today."

"Anna Jane are you excited about going to school for the first time?" Nathan asked as the children entered the schoolyard. He placed the ball in his pocket. He didn't want the teacher to take his new possession.

"Lila Ann says Mr. Wills is really nice," Anna Jane stopped to adjust her stockings before she entered the school building.

Nathan's eyes began to twinkle, "Anna Jane, did Lila Ann tell you that Mr. Wills has a big thick hickory limb that he keeps under his desk?"

Anna Jane stopped and froze on the steps with her eyes becoming wider and her mouth dropping open. Just the effect Nathan looked for when he continued, "And he uses it across your behind, three hard strokes if you don't behave yourself!"

"Nathan Laboree, you stop that! You are scaring Anna Jane to death," Lila Ann came up beside Nathan to slap him on the shoulder.

Joe Henry walked over to his younger brother and grabbed his head placing it under his arm. He began to rub his knuckles hard into the top of Nathan's head, "Yeah, stop scaring your cousin or I'll tell Mr. Wills you called him a bow-legged bull frog!"

"A bow-legged what did you say?" Mr. Wills appeared at the doorway grinning. Robert Wills stood 5' 9" tall, a slender, clean-shaven man who had slightly balding blonde hair. He had a long strand of hair on the right side of his head that he combed across the top of his head to cover the bald spot. He rarely raised his voice, but his piecing blue eyes could scream at you if he fixed them in your direction.

Both boys snapped to attention, staring straight up at their teacher, this time their mouths opened in surprise. Mr. Wills only chuckled, "I never bring Ole Hickory out unless you have really misbehaved. I don't think I've ever had to use it on either of you Laboree boys."

Now, who do we have here?" Mr. Wills turned to look at Anna Jane who stood very still with her mouth still open and eyes staring. Mr. Wills stepped over and taking his finger gently closed Anna Jane's mouth. "Are you Lila Ann's little sister?"

Lila Ann still looked angrily at her cousin as she turned to respond to her teacher, "Yes, Mr. Wills, this is Anna Jane."

"Well, Miss Anna Jane Ireland, won't you come in and I'll find you a seat right up front," Robert Wills gently took Anna Jane's hand as he led her into the schoolhouse. Lila Ann and the cousins followed. Everyone in the room turned to look as the group walked down the center row of student desks. Joe Henry, Nathan, and then Lila Ann found their assigned seats.

Before escorting Anna Jane to her seat Mr. Wills placed his hands one on each of her shoulders and turned her to face the class. "Class, this is Miss Anna Jane Ireland, Lila Ann's little sister. Will you please welcome her to our class?" This made Anna Jane feel very special and each of her cheeks glowed a little pinker than they usually did.

"Hello, Anna Jane," the class said in unison even Nathan joined in because he felt a little ashamed for scaring Anna Jane so much.

The morning went quickly with several of the older groups of children practicing for the Friday afternoon parent-teacher program. Every first Friday of the month Robert Wills had a meeting for parents. Robert knew that a lot of the parents could not read or write and he liked to get them involved as much as he could. The children did recitations, spelling bees, reading and other entertainment especially during any holidays.

Mr. Wills checked his pocket watch and started toward the door with a large hand bell in his hand. As he started ringing the bell the students began grabbing lunch buckets and scurrying toward the warm sunny day that awaited them outside. The older boys, led by Joe Henry, hardly took time to eat. They all gathered around Nathan, excited by the new baseball that had appeared from his pocket.

Lila Ann and her best friend, Mary found a low comfortable log where they could sit and eat their lunch without being disturbed by other children. Mary knew Anna Jane from her visits to the Ireland house during the summer. Lila Ann had waited impatiently all morning to get time at lunch to tell Mary her exciting news about the fire at the McCall cabin.

"It was the biggest fire that I have ever seen," Lila Ann began, "The smoke curled up the side of the mountain and woke us all up. It even made my eyes burn! And when the roof caved in the flames shot up. The flames got higher than some of the tall pine trees."

"Wow! Was your Pappy there?" Mary's dark almost black eyes glowed big and round. She had long thick black hair and a dark complexion. Mary's mother and father came from the Native American tribe called the Cherokee. Mary's parents lived about one hundred miles from the little mountain community. They had moved to it when her father got a job working on the railroad. Lila Ann loved to listen to her friend tell about this Indian Reservation her family came from. Charles Ireland's grandmother, Lila Ann's great-grandmother had been Cherokee. Lila Ann felt a kinship to Mary because of this. She also tried to protect Mary when some of the children would pick on her because they considered Indians evil.

"Pappy helped to put out the fire," Lila Ann boasted.

Anna Jane added, "Pappy's a hero!"

Lila Ann frowned as she bit into her biscuit. She had picked up on the feelings of her parents, that something just wasn't right about that whole situation. It bothered Lila Ann.

Mr. Wills came to the door ringing the hand bell to let the students know that lunch and recess had finished, time to continue the school day. Anna Jane jumped off of the log so quickly Lila Ann and Mary almost got dumped on the ground.

"Whooooo," Mary exclaimed catching herself, "Where is Anna Jane going in such a hurry?"

"Oh, she is excited about her first book, the First Reader that Mr. Wills gave her this morning. She thinks she will be able to go home this evening and read it to Mommy and Pappy."

Mary and Lila Ann headed for the school and had just gotten to the door when they heard a loud noise behind them. Joe Henry and Tommy Stewart rolled on the ground punching and kicking. All the children started gathering around them encouraging the fight. Mary turned to Lila Ann, "What has gotten into Joe Henry? I've never seen him this mad. And Tommy Stewart is older and bigger than him. Where is his mind?"

Before Lila Ann could reply Mr. Wills came out of the school and down the steps to grab each boy and pull them apart. A bit of blood trickled down Joe Henry's mouth but he didn't seem to notice. He strained toward Tommy and Tommy just smirked back at him. Robert Wills shook Joe Henry's arm and turned him so Joe Henry would have to look at his teacher instead of Tommy.

"Joe Henry, stop this right now! What on earth has gotten into you? You have never acted this way before."

Before Joe Henry could answer Tommy responded, "I just told Joe Henry his uncle was a fire starter. The talk is that Charles Ireland set that fire at the McCall cabin so no one else could live there and he could sharecrop that land. The sheriff is investigating, I heard. Joe Henry jumped me like a wild cat!"

"That's a lie, Tommy Stewart! You're a bald face liar!" Joe Henry struggled against Robert Wills' hold on him.

Anna Jane appeared at the door of the school just in time to hear Tommy's little speech. She immediately burst into tears. "My Pappy is a hero! He helped to put out that fire, not start it!" Looking to her sister she replied, "Tell them, Lila Ann! He didn't start that fire!"

Lila Ann turned to the group; all eyes waiting for her response, but as if time had stopped she couldn't get anything in her body to work especially her mouth. In her mind she wondered how anyone could blame her Pappy for such a horrible act.

Lila Ann stood there for a few more seconds wanting so hard to punch that smirk right off of Tommy Stewart's face. Then mustering all of the courage she had in her with her heart beating wildly she opened her mouth and calmly spoke, "My Pappy has no reason to set fire to that cabin. The McCalls are our friends and they have gone. My Pappy doesn't need that farmland to plant. Zeb Cox owns that property and Pappy has no fight with him. My Pappy is an honest man and loves my Mommy, my brother, my sister and me."

With that said and silent tears rolling down her cheeks, Lila Ann took her sister by the hand, picked up her dinner bucket and headed for the path that led home. She did feel as soon as the words came out that she did not have to stay and hear any more of this rubbish from any of them. Her heart filled with pride as she walked away from her cousin, Joe Henry, who knew no fear when defending his cousin's good name and someday she would tell him so......

As Lila Ann and Anna Jane disappeared into the woods, Robert Wills turned his attention back to the boys. First turning to Tommy Stewart he said, "Tommy Stewart, at fourteen I am not required to have you here. You are invited to leave and stay home. This is not the first time you have caused a commotion at this school. I believe I have taught you all that you are able to learn. This school does not go beyond the seventh grade. Leave and if I catch you back on the school grounds I will summon the sheriff, myself, to have you escorted off!

Without saying another word Tommy dusted off his clothes and stomped off in the direction of Cox's store. Robert then turned a gentler and, yet firm attention to Joe Henry, he said, "Joe Henry, I think it is admirable that you would so valiantly defend your cousin's good name but I must protest the brute force with which you chose to do it. Violence is never the answer. In the future you need to take heed of that."

"Yes, sir," Joe Henry replied realizing he had blood on his mouth he took his sleeve to wipe it away.

"Come over to the well and we'll clean you up," Robert said and turning to his audience still watching with mouths open, "I don't see how we can continue class after all this commotion. Class is dismissed until early tomorrow morning."

This sent giggling, screaming children in all directions and left Robert Wills, Nathan, and Joe Henry alone at the well to talk.

CHAPTER 4
THE GRANDFATHER

As the girls entered the clearing of the Laboree farm, a striking figure with silver hair and a long silver beard sat on the front porch of the house talking to Willie. John Laboree, not a big man by statue, had dark twinkling eyes and a warm smile that commanded attention. Even though he left his mother country, France, when only a boy of fifteen, he still had a heavy French accent. John turned his attention from his grandson to the two little girls as they entered the yard. Willie greeted the girls with a question, "What are you girls doing home so early? Is something wrong?" Willie's concern brought him to his feet. "Where are Nathan and Joe Henry?"

Lila Ann stopped and so did Anna Jane who was following her; she didn't really feel like answering questions. She just wanted to go home and talk to her Mommy and Pappy and figure this whole thing out. But she also realized she had to answer Willie's question, "I got upset, and that's all. Joe Henry got into a fight with Tommy Stewart and Mr. Wills sent Tommy home. Joe Henry and Nathan should be along soon."

Lila Ann took Anna Jane's hand and started toward her cabin when the Grandfather got up to stand next to Willie on the porch flashing a charming smile he said, "Bonjour, petit Mademoiselles." Turning to Willie he asked, "Are these your cousins, Charles and Lockie's girls?" Willie grinned and nodded yes.

Even though Lila Ann did not know French and had never met John Laboree, she had heard many stories of him from Joe Henry. She had heard about his organ grinder and the little monkey that entertained the family and the community for many years before she was born. She remembered the special trip with Joe Henry and Nathan to the family cemetery high on top of the mountain above their house to see the grave of the "petit" monkey and the little wooden grave marker with that inscribed on it. Joe Henry had tried many times to imitate his grandfather's French accent. Lila Ann quickly realized this must be him and she stopped in her tracks to stare at him.

The Grandfather came down the steps and approached the girls still flashing that charming smile. Willie joined him and made the introduction, "Grandfather Laboree, this is Lila Ann and, Anna Jane Ireland. They are my first cousins that live in the little cabin down the road."

Taking each little girl's hand, the Grandfather gently kissed each hand and replied, "It is my pleasure to meet you, Lila Ann and Anna Jane, tres bon!"

Lila Ann and Anna Jane had never been greeted in such a way and they both at the same time looked down at their hands and then back at the Grandfather. This reaction got Willie so tickled he chuckled out loud. He couldn't wait for his girlfriend Cindy to meet his grandfather and see her reaction to his charm.

The Grandfather well into his eighties and still an attractive man didn't have the heart to charm many people since his beloved Claudine had passed. He lived with his oldest son down in the Piedmont of North Carolina now and didn't travel as much as he did when he was younger. This farmhouse was one that he had built for his young bride so many years ago. When she had passed twenty years before, he had wanted to leave it and the sorrow of missing her.

Fate had asked to move into this house when he married Ora and the Grandfather graciously gave it to them as a wedding gift. This had been a happy place for John Laboree and as he came closer to the end of his life, he wanted to return to it to capture some of those memories.

Lila Ann was so taken by the Grandfather's charms and real French accent, she almost forgot about her troubles.

"Are you the Frenchman, the one that had the monkey and the organ grinder?"

"The very one, I use to live in this house and I am the one who built it for your Uncle Fate's mother."

"Did you really have a monkey and organ grinder?"

"Oui, I mean yes, I did. Did Joe Henry tell you about that?"

"He took me to see the little monkey's grave up on the mountain last summer."

As the Grandfather talked to his cousins, Willie scanned the woods wondering about the so called fight that Joe Henry had with Tommy Stewart and why they would even be fighting in the first place, when he noticed someone standing just at the edge of the woods near the path to school. It was a child and he wouldn't have noticed the child if he hadn't been looking for his brothers. It was a little girl with long dark hair, a dark child he had never seen before. "Hey, hello, you there, hello, who are you looking for?"

Everyone stopped talking and looked to see what or who had caught Willie's attention. Lila Ann immediately recognized her friend, Mary and ran over to greet her.

"What happened? Is everything all right?" Lila Ann asked as she pulled Mary into the yard and toward the others.

"I guess. Mr. Wills let school out after he told Tommy Stewart off and told him never to come to school again or he'd call the sheriff. I think he dismissed school early so he could talk to Joe Henry and Nathan without everyone else listening. He didn't seem too mad at them. I was worried about you so I came to find you." Mary said.

"Oh, Mary, I don't understand what is going on. I just wanted to go home and talk to Mommy and Pappy. And I especially didn't want to hear the others teasing me. You know how some of them are."

"Yes, I most definitely do. You have come to my rescue many times. They love to tease me cause I'm different from them." Mary said as she hung her head down. "That is why I came to make sure you were all right but now that I see you are fine, I must go back and go home. My Mother will worry if I'm late."

"I need to go home too, but wait, Joe Hency's grandfather is here. You have heard some of the stories Joe Henry told of him, haven't you? Our troubles can wait a little while, come and meet him. Listen to him talk. He is very different too." Lila Ann said as she pulled Mary over to the house and the porch where the Grandfather had gone back to sit down again.

Just as Lila Ann and Mary started up the porch steps, Joe Henry and Nathan appeared from the path in the woods. "Hey, Lila Ann, that was a grand exit you and Anna Jane made from school. But you both missed Mr. Wills telling Tommy Stewart to go home and never come back!"

"Yes, he told old Tommy if he ever came back to school he would notify the sheriff, himself and have him escorted off the school property!" Nathan chimed in.

"Don't you worry any about your Pappy. Mr. Wills said he would be over later to talk to Uncle Charles." Joe Henry said and looked up toward his house. There on the porch with Lila Ann and Willie sat the man he most admired in all of his life, his grandfather.

"Grandfather Laboree! When did you get here?" Both boys made a mad dash to greet him.

Willie interrupted Joe Henry's greeting to his grandfather, "What is this about you getting into a fight at school?"

"Willie, can this not wait until later? I have not seen Joe Henry since he was three years old and this red hair, you must be Nathan, tres bon!" the Grandfather said taking Nathan's face in both hands, "Just look at that curly red hair! Your mother's Scotch-Irish ancestors, I see!"

The Grandfather hugged both boys close to him. Then looked up to notice the new little dark haired stranger, Mary. "Ahhhhh, another petit Mademoiselle, and who might this be?" he said reaching for her hand.

Lila Ann stepped up to make the introductions, "Grandfather Laboree, this is Mary Maney, my best friend from school."

Anna Jane added, "Mary is an Indian."

"Je voir, I see," the Grandfather gently kissed Mary's hand and got the same reaction that he had from Lila Ann and Anna Jane.

"That's how a Frenchman greets women," Lila Ann whispered in Mary's ear.

"What is the name of your tribe?" the Grandfather asked Mary as they all sat down on the steps to visit and even Willie sat down because of his fascination with the Grandfather.

"I am a Cherokee."

"Ah, oui, I mean yes. In my travels out west when I was young I also met many Cherokee."

"Yes, my ancestors did not go when the government removed Cherokee from the reservation in the mountains. My great-grandfather owned his land in the Qualia Boundary. The government took it away from him. When they formed the new reservation my great-grandfather trusted them. Not long after they moved to it he was told they would move again to a reservation in the west. My great-grandfather decided not to go because he loved these mountains so much but hid out in these mountains with his family. Some of his children married into white families. He also had good friends among some of the white men who lived near him. Many in his tribe were not so lucky."

"My Cherokee friends in Oklahoma called that trip from these mountains The Trail of Tears because so many Cherokee died on the way to Oklahoma," the Grandfather shook his head, "It is sad the way the government has treated the Indians in this country."

"The government sent my father to Pennsylvania to Carlisle School when he was a boy to teach him the white man ways. He and his family were forbidden to speak our Cherokee language."

"I have heard the Cherokee language spoken and it is a beautiful language like my native French, oui!"

"My grandmother taught me Cherokee before we left the reservation that was re-established here in these mountains. I miss her very much. She passed away last spring right after my father, my mother, and I left so my father could work on the railroad. There is not much work for the Cherokee around the reservation and we were very poor," Mary hung her head down.

"Oh, beau enfant, that is, beautiful child, you are among friends here! And you are very welcome here at my son's home and so are your parents!"

"I really need to go home now before it gets too late. It is so nice to meet Joe Henry's grandfather! Joe Henry has told us many stories about you," Mary said as she started to walk back toward the path to school. "I will see you tomorrow, Lila Ann, and you too, Anna Jane!"

Lila Ann and Anna Jane ran to hug Mary before she disappeared into the woods. Lila Ann turned to her relatives on the porch and smiled. She longed to stay longer and just listen to the Grandfather but her mind flooded with memories of the afternoon and she knew she needed to head home.

"I really need to go home too and talk to Mommy and Pappy," she said as she picked up her dinner bucket and reached for Anna Jane's hand, "We will see you again soon, won't we?"

"Oui, yes, sweet cousin, I will be visiting for a while." Then the Grandfather turned to talk to his grandsons, he didn't tell them he had come home to stay. The Grandfather did not want them to know that he felt in poor health and had come home to die. He wanted to be in the place that he loved most near his beloved wife buried up on the mountaintop when that time came.

CHAPTER 5
THE ARREST

Lila Ann and Anna Jane came walking into the yard of their home about the time of day that they normally would have because of their visit with the Grandfather, so Lockie had no way of knowing all that had taken place that day at school. She came out on the porch holding little Jimmy's hand as the girls got to the foot of the steps.

"Well, how was your first day at school, Miss Anna Jane?"

Lila Ann and Anna Jane just looked at each other and then back at their mother. Lila Ann's mind raced, where would she begin? Anna Jane spoke first, though, "Mommy, did Pappy set fire to the McCall house? Tommy Stewart said he did and he said the sheriff was in.... inve.... invest ...”

"Investigating," Lila Ann continued, "Joe Henry got into a fight with Tommy Stewart because of what he said about Pappy. Mr. Wills broke up the fight and told Tommy to never come back to school again or he'd have the sheriff make him leave!"

"And Joe Henry's grandfather is here to visit and we got to meet him and he kissed my hand," Anna Jane held up the hand that the Grandfather had kissed and catching her breath she added, "I got my First Reader and I really like Mr. Wills and there are some Cherokees out West and some Cherokees here in these mountains," Anna Jane finished with a smile.

Lockie just stood there listening, eyes wide, mouth open while holding Jimmy's hand. Charles had heard the girls talking as he walked around the side of the cabin, taking in Anna Jane's entire continuous rendition of the day's events. For several minutes the little family just stood frozen in time, when finally Lockie spoke, "Well, my goodness, it has been quite a day for everyone, hasn't it?"

Lockie then turned to look at Charles, "I guess we need to discuss this problem with the girls, don't we, Charles?"

"Yes, now would be a good time. And did you know that John Laboree was coming home?"

"No, Ora never said a word the last time I was there," Lockie's feet were starting to ache so she led Jimmy over to the steps and sat down.

"Neither did Fate. I think something is wrong." Charles walked over to the girls placing his hands on their shoulders, "Come over here girls and let's talk about this very interesting day. Let's discuss this situation with the McCall cabin. First, I didn't set that fire."

"That is what I told everybody at school today when Mr. Wills broke up the fight. I told them you are a good man, Pappy," Lila Ann interrupted.

"Boy, I've never seen Joe Henry so mad. If Mr. Wills hadn't pulled him off of Tommy I think Joe Henry could have beaten him up good!" Anna Jane exclaimed.

"Well," Lockie chimed in, "I don't think it was a very good first day of school for Anna Jane to see a fight. It isn't like Joe Henry to use violence that way either. Although, if I had been there and heard that said about your Pappy I would have wanted to hit Tommy too!" Lockie rubbed her swollen ankles.

"I felt that way too when I told everyone what I thought and I just didn't want to hear anymore things said. I just wanted to come home and talk to you and Pappy about this. I didn't get to hear Mr. Wills tell Tommy off either but Mary Maney came to see about me and she found us at Joe Henry's house meeting the Grandfather. She also told us about school being dismissed early."

"Mary Maney, so that is where the Cherokee thing came into this ....” Charles smiled, "But one thing at a time, back to this cabin fire."

"And have you both been at Joe Henry's since you left school?" Lockie interrupted.

"Yes, we met Joe Henry's grandfather on our way home. Mary Maney came there while we were there and met him too."

"He kissed Mary's hand too," Anna Jane said looking at the hand he kissed again.

"Is Joe Henry all right?" Lockie asked.

"He looked all right to me when he came home a while ago," Lila Ann was still very worried about her Pappy, "Will the sheriff come and arrest you, Pappy?"

"I don't know, Lila Ann, I really don't know but I sure didn't start that fire. Someone did, though. And Zeb Cox had it done because he offered me money to do it. And I sure didn't ask him why he wanted it done, I just told him no. Who knows, Zeb may have started that fire himself since I turned him down. And I don't know how I'd prove that or even convince the sheriff of that."

"But, Pappy, you were a hero! You helped to put out that fire and I told them at school today that too!" Anna Jane said.

Charles rubbed the top of Anna Jane's curly brown hair, "I know, bright eyes, I know. Don't you girls worry.

I'll take care of it so don't worry," Charles pulled Jimmy over into his lap," Now, tell me and your Mommy about Joe Henry's grandfather, the Frenchman."

"Where is Mary Maney if she followed you home to check on you?" Lockie asked looking around for her.

"She went home after she met the Grandfather

"So I assume that is where the discussion came in about the Cherokee with the Grandfather?" Charles said as he bounced Jimmy up and down on the end of his foot. Jimmy giggled and held onto his Pappy's leg.

"The Grandfather told us he had been out West when Mary told him that she was a Cherokee. He said that many years ago when he was young he had been in Oklahoma and there were Cherokee there too. Mary said that her ancestors didn't go out West on a Trail of Tears but stayed here in the mountains hiding. The Grandfather said the government made most of the Cherokee go out to the West. And some of them hid and didn't go and many of the Cherokee died that went out West, which is why they called it the Trail of Tears.

"Mary said she was born on a new rese .... reser..... reserva.... "

"Reservation, Anna Jane new reservation here in these mountains," Lila Ann finished.

"Well, I need to get supper ready," Lockie said as she pulled herself up from the porch, "Girls take Jimmy out to play, won't you?"

"Yes'um," the girls said together.

"Lockie, I'm going to walk the girls to school tomorrow. I need to check into this matter and also pay a visit to John Laboree," Charles said but little did he know that his plans would never happen.

That evening with the children asleep, Lockie and Charles had gone out on the back porch to talk about the problem and what they were going to do about the sheriff. The sound of horses interrupted their conversation. Charles walked to the end of the back porch so he could see around the side of the house. He saw his brother-in-law, Fate riding with the group.

"We are around back," he hollered. He heard the scuffling of men and horses as the men dismounted, tied up the horses and came around the side of the house to the back porch where the couple stood.

Fate led the group with a gray-haired man Charles recognized as John Laboree. Following John was the children's schoolteacher, Robert Wills and right behind him was a dark-haired, dark-eyed man Charles didn't recognize at first until they got closer.

"Ed Maney, I didn't know you! And John Laboree, when did you get home? The girls told me about your visit. Robert Wills, are you all some kind of posse come to take me to jail or something?"

"Not exactly," Fate said, "but you're close. Charles, you need to get you some clothes and get ready to take a trip, quickly."

"What are you talking about?" Lockie came over and put her arm through her husband's arm.

"I'm sorry, Lockie, we don't have time for explanations right now. Tomorrow we will come and take you to the house to stay until that baby is born. We are here just ahead of the sheriff and we barely have time to get Charles out of here."

"Lila Ann told us what Tommy Stewart said at school and how Joe Henry got into a fight over it but I didn't think the story would lead to the sheriff really taking any action against Charles. How could they have any proof that Charles did anything and why would he do something like that, anyway?"

"I don't know, Lockie, I only know the sheriff decided to take action on Zeb's word. Zeb is a powerful man," Fate shook his head, "Now, come on Charles, we don't have much time. We got a horse for you and Ed is going to use his Cherokee sense of direction to take you toward the Virginia/Tennessee line."

Ed spoke up then, "I know someone in Virginia who will give you a job. After Lockie has the baby she and the children can join you."

Charles and Lockie looked at each other and Lockie shuttered, as she said, "Charles, I can't stand the thought of having this baby without you with me!" Lockie knew it was going to be a rough fall as she began to cry softly.

Charles hugged Lockie close, "Don't worry, Lockie, you'll have a house full of family to see you through this. I'll be there with you in my heart and my mind. And as soon as you're able to travel you and the young'uns will be with me again."

CHAPTER 6
THE WEDDING

Lila Ann awoke the next morning and got up to start getting ready for school. Her mother usually woke her up especially on school mornings. As Lila Ann slipped into her clothes she could hear someone very softly crying on the back porch. She quickly turned around to see if Anna Jane had stirred in her bed yet and saw both she and Jimmy sleeping soundly. She then realized that it must be her mother. She finished dressing and slipped to the back porch.

"Mommy, are you all right?"

Lockie jerked up the end of her apron when she realized one of the children had gotten up and quickly wiped her eyes. She had prepared a little speech in her mind as she sat alone on the back porch and now she had to deliver it. She felt alone and frightened for the first time in her life but she knew she had to hold up for her children and the unborn child she would soon bring into the world.

"I'm fine, dear. I just have dust in my eyes. Are Anna Jane and Jimmy awake yet? If they aren't, will you get them up for me? I will get up from here and get breakfast started."

"Yes'um," Lila Ann said. She realized she hadn't seen or heard her father at all this morning, which was very unusual. "Mommy, where is Pappy? Did he go to Uncle Fate's already this morning?"

"No, Lila Ann, so get Anna Jane and Jimmy up for me. After breakfast we can talk about your Pappy and where he has gone."

"Yes'um," Lila Ann wondered. If the dream she had about horses and riders with a lot of men around the house had been a dream after all as she went to get her brother and sister out of bed.

Lila Ann and Anna Jane came into the kitchen with Anna Jane still rubbing her eyes. Lockie placed two steaming bowls of mush, which is cooked corn meal, in front of the girls along with glasses of milk. She settled Jimmy down in his chair with his mush that she had cooled some by putting more milk in it. Pouring herself a cup of coffee, she sat down across from her children. She studied each of her children intently. They were pretty children with a mixture of both her and Charles. She loved them dearly and noticed how big Lila Ann had gotten this summer. She had begun to look more like a young lady than a little girl.

"Do you remember those things that Tommy Stewart was telling Joe Henry about your Pappy and the fire and the sheriff investigating?" Both girls nodded and Jimmy just said, "Pappy gone."

"Yes, Jimmy, Pappy had to go somewhere," Lockie said with a tear in her eye, which she quickly wiped away. "Well, Tommy wasn't lying about the sheriff. Late last night after you were asleep Uncle Fate, the Grandfather, Mr. Wills, and Mary's father, Ed Maney came to help your Pappy leave before the sheriff got here to arrest him for setting fire to the McCall cabin. Now, I know your Pappy didn't do it but it was his word against Zeb Cox's and, well, Zeb is a wealthy man and all. Anyway, Ed Maney knew someone in Virginia that will give Pappy a job and we will join him as soon as this baby is born."

Anna Jane started crying and because she was crying Jimmy did too and when Anna Jane cried, "I want my Pappy," so did Jimmy. Lila Ann put her arm around Anna Jane and Lockie got up to put Jimmy in her lap to comfort him.

"Now, Anna Jane, your Pappy would be upset if he could hear you and Jimmy taking on so! You need to be strong and go to school and not let on that anything is wrong, you hear? Mr. Wills helped your Pappy with Uncle Fate so I don't think he will allow the children to discuss anything about this at school so you should have no problems there. You've got to be strong, we all do. Today while you are at school Fate, Ora and Willie are coming to help move our things to their house. It will be a bit crowded but we will be fine. Rose has said we can use her room cause she is staying at the Wilson's and she will be getting married next month. What with the wedding and this new baby, why, we are going to have our hands full! It will be time to see your Pappy again before you know it!"

Lockie even felt better after her little talk with her children. Anna Jane snubbed a little but did finally stop crying. The idea of a wedding and a new baby did sound very exciting indeed. Lila Ann even started to get a little excited with her Pappy safely away and the thought of being around the Grandfather all sounded like a big adventure. Anna Jane slid out of her chair to go to her mother and Jimmy and hug them and Lila Ann joined them.

Lila Ann looked up at her mother and said, "I'm going to miss my Pappy so much! Do you think we can be back together by Christmas, Mommy?"

"I should think if everything goes well with this baby, we should. Now, you best both get ready and get to school."

The girls scurried around and left with Jimmy and their Mommy eating breakfast. They were out the door and down the path to school. Joe Henry and Nathan were waiting for them on the porch along with the Grandfather. John Laboree got up to greet the girls when they walked into the clearing.

"How are my petit Mademoiselles this morning?"

"Good morning, we are fine," Lila Ann responded but Anna Jane only frowned. She missed her father and her cousins could see that. The Grandfather walked over and picked, Anna Jane up, which really surprised Lila Ann. She had never met another man like John Laboree who was so kind and caring except for her Pappy or maybe her Uncle Fate.

"My sweet Anna Jane, please don't be so sad. Your father is safe and you will both be together again real soon. After school when you come home with your cousins we will play some music because I've brought my organ grinder down from the attic just for you. It still makes wonderful music. I don't have my petit monkey but maybe we can get Nathan here to fill in for it."

Nathan started jumping around making funny monkey sounds and scratching under his arms, which made everyone laugh.

Anna Jane gave the Grandfather a big hug, "May I call you Grandfather too, even though you are not my real grandfather?"

"Oui, yes you may. I will consider you and Lila Ann my new adopted grandchildren." Sitting Anna Jane down he said, "Now, hurry on to school all of you so you will not be late."

The cousins all headed out to school with dinner buckets and books. Things at the Laboree farm would be in a flurry for the next several weeks, that day especially. The men worked all day moving Lockie's things into the house. They stored what furniture the Ireland's had in Fate's workshop in the barn, especially the prized new cook stove. Rose and Tom, her husband-to-be, had already gotten a house on the college campus where Tom worked so they had finished moving her things there. The next project would be the wedding itself that was planned in middle October. The leaves would be in their most beautiful time and Indian summer, hopefully, would be settled in the mountains before the cold weather set in.

The Grandfather had his aches and pains as anyone would have at his age but he had not shared with the family that he had other reasons for coming home to the house he had built other than the wedding of his granddaughter. He didn't want to ruin the wedding but each morning he found it more difficult than the next to get up. He hoped and prayed that his illness stayed at bay until after Christmas. He sat in his room while the family bustled around him cleaning his organ grinder for when the children got home from school. He wanted so much to set Lockie and her children at ease and help them deal with the separation from their father.

About dinner time Ora appeared at his door, "Grandfather, dinner is ready," Ora noticed John's face for the first time since his arrival. "John are you feeling all right? You look kind of pale to me."

John looked up at Ora and smiled. She looked to him much as she did when she married his son, a very handsome woman. Her auburn hair twisted in a braid at her neck reminded John of his wife, Claudine. How he still missed her and being in the house they had shared a life which brought back so many memories.

"I'm fine just still tired from the trip. It takes a day or two to hit me."

"Are you really going to play that organ grinder tonight? My goodness, Fate will have to break out the fiddle and maybe we can get Lockie to sing."

"I'll go get washed up and be into dinner. How is Lockie holding up with Charles gone?"

"Oh, she'll be fine. What with the moving and getting settled and then the wedding, we'll keep her laughing and busy. And after the wedding, that baby will be due." Ora turned to go back downstairs with John following behind her.

That evening after the Ireland family were settled in and supper had been served and cleaned up the family settled on the front porch on the warm September evening to make music. As the Grandfather played the organ grinder he described his little monkey, "My petit monkey loved the music. I think she had danced to it since she was a small baby. Whenever I brought the monkey into the house my Claudine would pin a diaper on her just like a petit baby!"

Everyone laughed at that description, "And Claudine had made the monkey a little red jacket. Now, that she did not mind wearing but the diaper she only tolerated it.

When I brought her outside she always found a way to get the diaper off."

The month went quickly and the days got shorter. The air had coolness to it now. The final plans for the wedding had begun and everyone grew more and more excited. The day of the wedding had arrived and Lockie bustled around as much as she could in her condition. She had promised to sing but she grew more nervous with just the thought of all the people that were suppose to be there many of whom she did not know.

"Oh, Ora, I'll loose my voice! I just know I will! And I'm so big when this baby moves it almost takes my breath away!"

"Now, Lockie, you'11 be fine. You look beautiful. There is always this glow around a pregnant woman. You are so full of life."

"I know what you can do," the Grandfather appeared at the door, "Open this letter from Charles Ireland. I bet that will put some notes in your voice."

"There is a letter from Charles? Oh my," Lockie felt faint and sat down in a chair as John handed the letter to her. It was postmarked Virginia nearly two weeks before.

"It sure took long enough to get here. I'm almost afraid to open it."

"Come on, read that letter and then you and I will go on the back porch and you can sing for just me and work the kinks out of your voice," the Grandfather reached for her hand and kissed it.

Lockie read the letter out loud. Charles was fine and he liked his job. Everyone had been very nice to him. And he found a nice small house that was furnished. He hoped they were fine and he missed them so much. He also missed the mountains, his mountains. When Lockie read that she choked up and started crying.

"Lockie, now stop that. You know he is safe and he has a place ready for you and the young'uns and as soon as that baby comes you'll go and be with him. Now, come on, we have a wedding to do." Ora turned and headed for the kitchen to make final preparations there.

The Grandfather placed his arm around Lockie and they headed for the back porch to practice. In the meantime, the girls were in the bedroom with Rose. Lila Ann was so enamored with her cousin Rose that she could not take her eyes off of her. The Grandfather had found something else when he went to the attic that day to get his organ grinder, a very special dress that had belonged to his Claudine, her wedding dress. She had so carefully placed it in a protected garment bag the store had given her when she had it made, when John found it, it was just as she had placed it nearly sixty years before. Rose had squealed when he brought it out to give to her. It was perfect with a little cleaning and adjusting here and there. Rose looked like a princess in it. John thought she looked a lot like Claudine with her dark hair and blue eyes. It bought tears to his eyes.

When a knock sounded at the Laboree's door, Rose responded quickly, "Oh, if that is Tom, he can't see me. It would be bad luck!"

Lila Ann went to the door and just barely cracked it to peer out, "Who is it?" To her surprise there stood Mary Maney.

"Your aunt told me it was all right to come up here. My mother and father are outside talking to your uncle. It really pleased them that we were invited. I have a very special gift for Rose, a wedding gift."

Mary extended a tissue-wrapped gift. Lila Ann grabbed Mary's arm with the present in it and pulled her into the bedroom.

"Oh, Rose, you are so beautiful," Mary said as she handed the gift to her.

"How sweet, thank you so much, Mary," Rose said as she sat down on the bed to open the gift.

She tore the white tissue from the gift revealing a shiny black vase with beautiful designs scratched into the sides of it. It had a handle in the middle with two separate openings on the top.

"How beautiful, I have never seen anything like it!" Rose said as she turned the vase and then looked into it.

"It is a very special vase. It is called the wedding vase and my grandmother made it. It is the black pottery. I used to help my grandmother make her pottery to sell on the reservation. The two separate openings are for the bride and groom to drink from after the wedding ceremony the bride drinks from one side and the groom the other for good luck."

Rose reached over and pulled Mary to hug her and said, "This is the most special gift I have ever received. It will be an honor to use this when we cut the cake. Lila Ann, take this down to my mama and tell her when we are to have it. Thank you again, Mary. Now, I'd better get everything together. Will you girls help me?"

The day of the wedding arrived and the plan to have the wedding outside if the weather allowed had been Rose's and so far the weather had been perfect. The trees were all colors and the air grew warm as it did in Indian summer. The sky had a magnificent blue and that made the reds, yellows, greens, oranges, and even the browns brighter. Lockies's mellow voice floated through the air as the bride on the arm of her handsome father marched through the yard to meet her Tom. Everyone would talk about the wedding for many weeks for it was perfect. For many months afterwards Lila Ann's dreams were filled with the images she saw this day only it would be her in her future wedding as a grown young woman. Also within the week as the weather began to tum cooler Lockie took to her bed with pains and the family braced itself for the next event, the new baby.

CHAPTER 7
THE NEW BABY

Joe Henry sat outside on the porch even though a cold wind blew. He just had to get out of that house! Nathan had gone to the store with Willie and their father and Joe Henry had decided not to go with them. He needed to think. His whole life seemed to always be in turmoil the last couple of months what with the ordeal with his cousins, his sister's wedding and now this new baby cousin! Most of it had to do with the women in his family. At his age he was trying hard to understand them. When he tried to talk to his father, Fate chuckled and rubbed the top of his head. Fate would say things like, "Women, you can't live with them and you can't live without them." What did that mean, Joe Henry wondered?

During the wedding he just tried to stay out of the way. He had new feelings and watching the wedding had stirred something in him. He had noticed some of the girls that were there. Honestly he thought, girls really got into this wedding thing. One girl really caught his attention, though. She went to his school and he had never noticed her before the wedding, her name was Mary Maney with the long dark hair and twinkling dark eyes. She and her parents had attended the wedding and brought a very special gift for his sister. Once she looked at him and smiled and her eyes twinkled so it looked like stars in the night sky. And her hair was like black silk. She wore it down loose and it went almost to her waist. He thought of the story that Mr. Wills had read to them at school about Pocahontas and John Smith. If that Indian princess had looked like Mary Maney no wonder there were stories written about her.

A wagon pulled up into the yard just then. The midwife, Jane had arrived. A midwife is usually a lady who helps to deliver babies when doctors are not available.

"Hello, Joe Henry, how are you today?"

"Hello, I'm fine, and you?"

"I'm fine too and I'm here to help your new cousin come into the world. It's a bit cold out here. Aren't you cold sitting out here on the porch?"

"A little, I reckon, just getting some air. Would you like me to show you where Aunt Lockie is?"

"Yes, sir, that would be very kind of you."

Joe Henry opened the door for Jane and led her up the stairs but he stopped short of the bedroom door. He left Jane to knock on it. When Ora stuck out her head he could hear a lot of moaning coming from Lockie and when pain got harder she would even holler a bit. He hurried back down the stairs. That was totally woman territory.

Several hours later the door opened and Joe Henry could hear a baby crying. Jane came down the stairs putting her coat back on and seeing Joe Henry standing at the foot of the stairs, she smiled and said, "You have a new cousin, a boy with strawberry blonde hair."

Fate, Nathan, and Willie entered from the kitchen just as Jane was opening the front door to leave.

"Did I hear a baby?" Fate asked.

Jane stopped with her hand on the door knob to reply, "Yes, Lockie and Charles have a new son, strong and healthy. He has strawberry blonde hair like his mother."

The Grandfather came in the front door, causing Jane to jump, "Did I hear you say it's a boy?"

"Yes, Lockie said that she and Charles had decided to call the baby, Aaron Mark, if it was a boy."

"That is two good Bible names. Jane come in the kitchen for a cup of coffee before you leave. And when you leave Willie will follow your wagon to make sure you have a safe trip home." Fate said and then took a roll of bills and pressed them into Jane's hand as they all walked into the kitchen.

"Grandfather, the women always have things going on. It seems like the men just have to stand back and wait on them," Joe Henry said later as he and his grandfather sat by the fire.

"I know it seems like that at times, Joe Henry. You '11 find the women have their times in the center of life and there will be times when the men are in the center of life too. It goes back and forth. Something tells me that you are beginning to notice women in a different light," the Grandfather smiled and hugged his grandson.

"Don't worry. Every man goes through this at your age. Tomorrow you and I are going to take a walk as soon as you get in from school and we'll talk more about this."

The next day things seemed to settle down a little around the Laboree farm after the birth of Lila Ann and Anna Jane's new brother. It started getting on toward evening when the sound of horses and men talking drifted up to the bedroom window where Lila Ann sat rocking her new baby brother. Anna Jane and Jimmy sat on the floor playing with some toys Fate had brought them from Cox's store. Lila Ann went to the window to look out after she took the baby to place him next to their mother.

"Who is that?" Lockie questioned.

Lila Ann had to look hard. There were several men outside and one looked very familiar. He talked to Uncle Fate and then they hugged, which she found very odd, then the man turned and looked up at the bedroom window.

"Pappy, it's my Pappy!" Lila Ann turned and ran out of the bedroom like a streak of lightning. She met her father in mid air halfway down the stairs. Charles caught her.

"Well, hello!" Charles chuckled and carried her into the bedroom with him. Before he got in the door two more children wrapped themselves around each leg, crying, "Pappy, Pappy!"

"I understand we have a new red-haired son," Charles said as he looked lovingly into his wife's eyes placing Lila Ann on the floor next to the others.

"Here, young'uns let your Pappy go so he can see this new baby."

The children went to stand at the end of the bed as Charles kissed his wife and took his new son from her arms. Looking down into the baby's tiny face he said, "Hello, Aaron Mark, it is a pleasure to meet you."

"Charles, how on earth did you know he was born yesterday?"

"You can thank John Laboree. He wired the company that I worked for and my boss not only loaned me the horse but he also sent some of his other men with me to make sure I had no trouble once I got here. I can't stay long, though. I miss you and the children so much, but I have to return to Virginia before anyone hears that I am around these mountains."

"There are still a few good people left in this world," Lockie said and smiled.

"I rode like the devil to get here and we'll need to let those horses rest and feed before we head back."

Ora appeared at the door, "Charles, it is you. I thought Nathan was pulling my leg when he said you were here. How on earth did you know this baby had been born?"

"You can thank your good father-in-law for that. He wired the company that I work for and let me know. I rode like the wind to get here and I'll have to get back soon before someone finds out I'm here and tells the sheriff."

"We can feed you and your friends before you leave and Fate and Willie can take those horses to the barn and rub them down, water and feed them. You and your friends can stay the night and leave before daybreak in the morning. I'll go get food started now," Ora said as she turned to Lila Ann, "Sweetie, come downstairs with me and help me, won't you? Since Rose is gone I sure could use your help."

Lila Ann ran over to hug her Pappy and said, "Yes'um, Aunt Ora, I'd be glad to."

Charles walked over to catch Ora's hand while still holding his son in the other, "Ora, I will never be able to repay you and Fate for all you have done. Thank you so much!"

"Don't think nothing of it, you are family and you are most welcome," Ora said patting Charles on the back.

Before daybreak Charles and Lockie talked about the planned trip for her and the children to Virginia before he left to return to his job. "Ora said I should be good to make the trip in about a month if the weather isn't bad. Fate said he would take us to Erwin, Tennessee to catch the train."

"That will be good. I will have the house ready when you come. I'm going to miss you and the young'uns so much. It is so strange when I come home and there is no one there. I hope I can stand it for another month. You take care and if you need me send a wire to my company. I love you!" Charles said as he hugged Lockie goodbye.

"The young'uns will be mad you didn't wake them"

"It breaks my heart to see them cry, Lockie. Tell them I love them, please."

As Charles went out the door Lockie replied, "I will, Charles." She turned her face into the pillow so he wouldn't hear her crying and she wouldn't wake the children.

CHAPTER 8
THE GHOST

The next morning, after the cousins left for school, Willie and Fate were on the back porch cleaning their guns. The fall of the year is an excellent time for hunting for the men of the mountains. It is a time also to check the hogs and take corn out to them. They had been turned loose in the unclaimed area of the mountains to fatten up. The hogs were taken when their young were six weeks old and left to fend for themselves eating mast that came from oak and chestnut trees. The hogs became a bit wide and grew long tusks.

"Come the coldest day in December before Christmas I think will be the time to round up those hogs for slaughter. They've been up near the Bald now for two years." Fate said.

Willie chuckled, "Remember the last time we had a round-up and Charles got treed by that hog with the long tusks?"

"Yeah, what really scared him, though, is when the hog started gnawing on the little tree that he climbed up on." Fate laughed, "If those dogs hadn't got to that hog and got its attention so I could shoot it, Charles said he could just feel those tusks on his throat."

Ora stepped out on the porch to bring Fate and Willie some hot coffee. "Have you noticed the Grandfather has been looking a little pale lately, Fate?"

"I've noticed he's been moving a little slower than he used to and sometimes his breathing sounds a little strange but he is eighty-four-years old. And he hasn't complained about feeling bad."

"I'm worried about him. You need to talk to him. He isn't one to complain even if he were sick. You know that."

"Where is he right now? I haven't seen him this morning."

"He's still in bed. He gets up later and later. It's like he has trouble getting up in the morning now."

"That isn't like my father. He was always an early riser. With all that has been going on I just haven't noticed him."

Fate put his gun down, "I'll go check him and we'll have a talk."

Fate walked into his father's room to find him washing up in the washbasin. "Ora is concerned you're not feeling well, Pa. Is everything all right?"

"I've not been feeling too good," John said as he dried his face, "I didn't want to be any trouble to anyone, what with the problems with Charles and then all the fuss with Rose's wedding. When I came home I figured it would be my last trip. I've lived a good life, Fate."

"Pa, we have a new doctor living near Cox's store. Would you have any problem letting a doctor come and check you out?"

"No, I wouldn't," John said as he and Fate went downstairs to breakfast.

That afternoon the cousins were at school. Lila Ann and Mary sat talking on their hollow log, while Anna Jane and her new friend, Nancy, were following Mr. Wills around. Lila Ann told Mary about her father's secret visit, "I sure wish Pappy had let Mommy wake us up before he left this morning. When Anna Jane got up she got really upset and cried and cried."

"That is probably why your Pappy didn't want to wake Anna Jane, Jimmy, and you up. Some people can't take the tears. I've noticed men don't like to cry, they think it is not manly," Mary wise beyond her twelve years noted. Her Cherokee grandmother had taught her many things besides making pottery. Mary wore her hair in one long braid down her back that day and it shined like pure silk. A not-so-new baseball suddenly pounced in front of the girls and landed at Mary's feet.

"Hello, how are you today, Mary?" Joe Henry said as he appeared almost in Mary's face to retrieve the ball.

"I'm fine, Joe Henry, and you?" Mary smiled and looked into Joe Henry's eyes.

Joe Henry seemed frozen in time as he just stood there taking in Mary's face and for a minute Lila Ann thought him to be dumb struck. Lila Ann just didn't know what to make of her cousin lately, he acted so strangely especially around her best friend. Suddenly the other boys started hollering at him and he snapped out of his trance, smiled at Mary and ran back to his game.

"I don't know what has gotten into Joe Henry. He seems to be a different person when he is around you now. He sure doesn't act like that at the house when we get home."

"My grandmother would say that it is his time to become a man. He has discovered girls and I guess he has found interest in me. I don't know why, though. It is all in a person's mind, who knows?"

Mr. Wills appeared at the door of the school and rang the bell. Being a little early for the bell, the boys fussed. The cold wind began to blow and the clouds began to gather. It looked like it might snow.

"Now, boys, stop your fussing. I thought it looked like snow and if it does start I may dismiss school early. I don't want the little ones to walk home in a bad snowstorm." Mr. Wills smiled when there was a low cheer from those same boys. Mr. Wills continued, "Let's continue with our lessons."

About two o'clock the snow started to come down pretty hard so Mr. Wills decided to go ahead and give them their homework and dismiss class. "The assignment I'm going to give to grades four through eight is due next Monday. I want you to write an interesting story about something you have heard about these mountains and the people in them. I call them Folk Tales. The young students need to practice their multiplication tables. Class dismissed and bundle up. It has turned cold out there, hurry home."

Mary wrapped her shawl tightly around her shoulders and head as she turned to Lila Ann to ask, "Lila Ann, what do you think you will write about?"

"I would like to write about when Mommy had her baby. It was very exciting or maybe about Rose and her wedding."

Joe Henry appeared, "Come on, Lila Ann, we need to get home. I want to talk to Grandfather about something," Joe Henry then turned to Mary, "I'll see you tomorrow, Mary. Be careful going home."

"Yes, Joe Henry, I will. Goodbye. See you both tomorrow."

As the cousins walked out the door, Lila Ann studied Joe Henry's face. He had a very little mustache starting to grow, she thought, or is that dirt on his upper lip? She didn't dare ask, instead she said, "You sure have developed an interest in my best friend, Mary, lately."

"She is a very pretty girl," Joe Henry seemed to grow uncomfortable and ran to catch up with his brother who had been tossing his baseball into the air as they walked home.

When the cousins got home Lila Ann and Anna Jane headed straight for their mother's room. The first thing they wanted to do after they got back from school was hold the baby and see who could get him to smile first. Joe Henry and Nathan went to find the Grandfather.

They found their grandfather sitting in the rocking chair in the front parlor watching the snowfall; Joe Henry found a good place on the floor in front of his grandfather and sat down with Nathan sitting down next to him. Joe Henry wanted to talk to his grandfather about his school project, and the Grandfather, he was sure, would have all the answers. He looked up into the Grandfather's face and asked, "What are you doing, grandfather?"

"Sitting here thinking about what I'm going to do with the rest of my life."

Joe Henry thought this an odd thing to say so he asked, "What do you mean?"

John Laboree looked down at his grandsons. He felt relief since he went to the doctor and the doctor had informed him that he had no serious illness. He told John to have Ora make him a good spring tonic in a couple of months. He realized he would have more time with his family and this made him feel so good. But with the puzzled looks on their faces, he knew he had better explain why he said what he did. They were old enough to understand.

"When I came here, boys, I felt sick and very old. I didn't just come to the wedding, I came home to die. I wanted to be here in the house that I built and lived in with your grandmother, Claudine. I have never been sick much in my life. I have been very fortunate. The doctor told me today that I had a little flux and gave me something for it but other than that I am fine. He told me to have your mom make me a good tonic in the spring, so I am sitting here thinking, what am I going to do with the rest of my life?"

Just then Ora came into the parlor carrying a cup of tea. "Here, grandfather, is some Spicewood tea. It is just the thing for the flux."

She smiled at her boys, what a sweet picture they all made sitting there by the fire. "There you boys are, I've been looking for you. You need to go see if your Pa needs some help getting those cows in the barn."

Before Joe Henry could complain the Grandfather said, "I think the boys need to talk to me," turning to the boys he said, "I have an idea. Go out and help your father and then after supper we will meet right here and we can talk then."

Ora smiled and said, "Thank you, John. That is an excellent suggestion."

After dinner the Grandfather had taken his place again by the fire with Joe Henry and Nathan at his feet. Joe Henry had brought along a pencil and paper to write things down. The Grandfather raised his eyebrows and commented, "Well, this looks serious."

"This is a project for school, grandfather. I have to write a story for school and I needed to ask you some questions to help me get started."

"What is your story about, Joe Henry?"

"Do you remember the story of the mountain girl that killed her husband and got hung for it? The one Pa always tells us haunts the woods up the road from here?"

"Yes, I do. Frances was her name and they called her Frankie. Their cabin set up above the ridge over across the road back in the 1830s. I heard the story of her when I first came to these mountains around 1850. I met her husband's family; in fact some of them still live down the road. Why don't you talk to some of them?"

"I have but they only have bad things to say about Frankie. None of her family are around to talk about it. They all left out after she got hung. They say her ghost is still around these parts. I never thought much about it until Willie went hunting over on that ridge last year. He and some of his friends camped out and ended up staying in a tree all night!"

"Why in a tree?" the Grandfather asked.

"They heard the most blood-curdling screams all night. They thought that could be the safest place until daybreak."

"Well, I've heard stories that others have told about hearing the screaming. That is interesting, indeed. Well, when I came to these mountains it had only been around twelve years since her hanging. Her brother still lived around here and he told me Frankie's story. He later went out west and got hung for horse stealing in Texas."

"Grandfather, tell us what he told of Frankie's story," Joe Henry and Nathan chimed in together.

"This is the story that Frankie's brother told to me."

It was a cold December night a few days before Christmas in 1832. Frankie and her husband, Charlie, lived in a little one-room cabin along with their two-year-old daughter, Nancy. Frankie was nineteen and Charlie was twenty. Frankie was a small thing that loved music and loved to dance. She was said to be a pretty little thing too. Charlie was a trapper and would go off on hunting trips with some of his neighbors and family members.

Sometimes they'd be gone for a week at a time. They lived just over the ridge from his family. Charlie's family had a lot of land and had given Charlie the land that he had built his cabin on. Frankie's family lived down the creek from them and her father was a sharecropper.

Charlie was known to drink some and usually got his spirits from a man down the road. During the holidays he was usually known to take a drink and take it with him when he went hunting. Charlie said the liquor helped the men to keep warm when they went trapping in the winter. He had cut a tree down that day so Frankie would have firewood while he was gone. He brought the axe in and sat it by the fireplace and got his bottle of liquor as he sat down to clean his rifle and prepare it for the hunt. He said that he needed some liquor to warm his bones after being out in the snow and cold all day.

Frankie was upset with him because he was going off and leaving her alone so close to Christmas. It was so lonely in the cabin with just her and little Nancy. Frankie got to fussing and complaining. The more she fussed, the more Charlie drank and the liquor made Charlie's temper flare. Directly they both started hollering at each other and the baby got upset and started to cry and cry and cry.

What with the baby's crying and Frankie's hollering, Charlie jumped up and yelled to the top of his lungs that if Frankie didn't hush that baby up, he would. And he pointed that rifle still in his hands at the baby. Well, the last time Frankie had seen Charlie that mad he had slapped her. Terror gripped Frankie's heart. She didn't know what Charlie wouldn't shoot the baby in a rage without thinking.

The rest was a reflex. Frankie spied the axe; it was the only thing in the house that she knew of could protect the baby and her so she grabbed it. Everything happened so quickly. Fear can give little people a lot of power and that's what it took for that little woman to swing that axe and she laid it right at an angle above Charlie's right ear.

It killed Charlie instantly. He never even knew what hit him. He just crumbled onto the floor with blood going everywhere. The minute it happened Frankie let go of the axe and ran to pick up the screaming baby. Then she slowly turned to take it all in. There in all the blood laid her dead husband that she had just killed. She got the baby hushed and just stood there for a long time, numb. The only thing she could think of was she had to clean up this mess before his family came to see it. What was she going to do in the middle of the night in a snowstorm?

She knew she couldn't do anything until she got Nancy to sleep so in the middle of all of the blood with her dead husband's body there on the floor she rocked the baby to sleep. Once Nancy was sleeping she laid her in her bed and got her boots and warm clothes on with a heavy shawl wrapped around her and headed out the door to her parent's cabin.

It was very late at night but she followed the creek that flowed right by her parent's cabin. It was the only thing she knew to do, to get some help from her family. When she got to her parent's cabin she had to beat on the door because they were all sound asleep and couldn't hear her. She was freezing when her brother finally opened the door to let her in.

Her mama rose up in bed to ask what on earth she was doing out in this weather in the middle of the night? Where were the baby and Charlie? Before Frankie answered any questions she asked where her pa was since she did not see him in bed with her mama.

Her mama explained that he and her older brother had gone off hunting for Christmas meat and would probably be back before Christmas day. Frankie only hung her head. Again her mama asked where the baby and Charlie were. Frankie looked up and said they were at the cabin and she started to cry.

Her mama then hit the floor grabbing her shawl to wrap around herself, while Frankie's brother worked on the fire to make the cabin a little warmer. Frankie's mama walked over and got Frankie by the shoulders and made her look up at her. *Frankie*, she said, *what has happened to Charlie and the baby? Why are you out here in the middle of the night alone in this cold?*

Frankie still crying told her mama that Nancy was asleep and then she started crying so hard she couldn't even talk. Her mama shook her hard and said, *what about Charlie, Frankie, what has happened to Charlie?*

Frankie's little brother found a clean rag and handed it to Frankie so she could wipe her nose. Frankie finally looked up at her mama and composed herself enough to tell her mama the awful truth. That Charlie lay dead on the floor of their cabin. Then Frankie cried harder and kept saying that she thought he was going to shoot the baby and her cause he was so mad. The axe was just there and she grabbed it and the next thing she remembered Charlie was dead there on the floor!

Frankie's mama looked at her little brother and he just looked back at her. They knew they had to get back to the cabin as soon as they could before one of the family came and found him. And especially before the baby woke up and realized she was alone in that cabin. They hurried and got dressed and left with Frankie in tow.

When Frankie's mama opened the door she was not prepared for what she saw. She caught her breath and nearly fainted. Her youngest child caught her and they both stood looking at the mess in the cabin in unbelief. Frankie pushed past her brother and mama and went immediately to her baby who was still sound asleep. Frankie, who was exhausted, lay down next to her baby and fell fast asleep. Her mama fetched a large braided rung to cover Charlie's lifeless body and then discuss with her son what they were going to do with the body. They decided they would burn it.

Frankie's mama told her brother to wake Frankie up that they would not clean her mess without her help. He gently woke Frankie so not to wake the baby. They each took turns cutting Charlie's body up because it would not fit in the fireplace as a whole. Frankie's mama fetched the large tub that they used to take a bath in and they placed the body with the wood that Charlie had spent the day chopping.

In the meantime, her brother was sent to the creek for water and Frankie's mama began the job of cleaning up the blood. They all worked through the wee hours of the morning until daybreak. Frankie's brother made many trips to the creek to dispose of the bloody water and fetch clean water until you could hardly tell that there had ever been any blood at all in that cabin.

Frankie's forehead and arms were full of sweat from working so close to the fire during the night. Her mama stepped over to see what was left in the tub. We won't be able to bum his lights, (the internal organs), so we best find a pouch to place them in and find a place to hide them when it gets light. She looked in the fireplace and saw his skull and some other bones that would not burn and got the fire poker and fished them out of the fireplace to place them in the tub with the other parts. Frankie's brother was given the job of disposing of them outside somewhere when it got daylight.

Frankie's mama then turned to Frankie and told her she was going home and taking the baby home with her. Then she told Frankie that she had better get down to Charlie's parents and let them know that Charlie had gone hunting. Have them come and feed the cow and then you come to the cabin to rest. This is on your shoulders, Frankie, I'll have no part of it if it gets found out, you hear?

Frankie did as she was told but she truly dreaded facing Charlie's parents. When she got down to their big log house over the ridge she found Charlie's stepmother and sisters washing clothes. They were never suspicious of anything Frankie told them that morning. Just the previous morning Charlie had told his father that he had planned to go hunting and that he was going home to cut wood for

Frankie to use while he was gone. Frankie told his stepmother that she was going to spend Christmas at her parent's cabin and would one of his brothers please see to feeding the cow for her? And Charlie's stepmother said she would.

A week passed and no one had seen Charlie or Frankie. The brother that had been feeding their cow commented that he had seen no sign of Charlie's footprints around the house that first morning that he went up there to feed the cow. He also commented that Charlie's dog was acting funny. Charlie always took that dog hunting with him. So Charlie's father decided that morning to go with his son to see what was going on around Charlie's cabin.

When they got to the cabin Charlie's father decided to go in and see if Charlie had been there and maybe gone on to Frankie's parents. When he got to the cabin door a strange very sour odor hit his face and his heart sank. He knew immediately something was terribly wrong. He decided to go find the sheriff of the county before he did anything else. The sheriff would know more about how to handle any wrongdoing. He was afraid to mess with anything that might be important to the investigation of his son's whereabouts.

Charlie's father went to the local country store to find the sheriff and while he was there he saw one of Charlie's hunting buddies. Charlie's friend informed him that "Charlie had never showed up for their hunting trip. And they had figured Charlie decided not to leave his family before Christmas. Now this really got Charlie's father upset, he knew something awful must have happened to his Charlie, his oldest son.

The sheriff came and looked around the cabin and then they went on to find Frankie at her parent's cabin. By that time Frankie's father and other brother had returned from their hunting trip. He wouldn't let them in to talk to Frankie. He told them that she was sick and, no, they had not seen Charlie and did not know what had become of him. They heard Frankie who had come to stand behind her father say that she didn't care if Charlie ever returned. Even though this made Charlie's father really upset the sheriff calmed him down and told him not to make a scene. He would deal with her later. They really needed to find Charlie or what had become of him first. They would return when they needed to return and question her.

Later that day after the sheriff went off to talk to more of Charlie's friends, his father got an idea. He had heard of a black conjure man who could find things with his crystal ball. That man lived just over in Tennessee, so Charlie's father saddled a horse and rode over to find him.

He took with him one of Charlie's shirts he had gotten from the cabin. He found the conjure man and paid a pretty penny to have him look into his crystal ball. The conjure man was the blackest black man that Charlie's father had ever seen. He had been a slave at one time and with all of the money he had made off of his gift he had purchased his freedom and also saved his master's life they told.

He held the shirt Charlie's father had brought for him that had been fetched out of the young couple's cabin for a moment and closed his eyes. Then he handed the shirt back to Charlie's father and looked into his crystal ball. He told Charlie's father that he would find his son close to his own cabin in several places and that was all he could see. By the time Charlie's father got back to the cabin Charlie's dog had found the skull in a hollow tree near the house. Charlie's brother had fetched the sheriff and they were ready to look more closely at the cabin.

They took the cabin apart and found the unusual greasy residue that later they realized was human flesh in the fireplace. When they pulled up the floorboards of the house they found bits of flesh and a lot of blood. There was no doubt in the sheriff's mind that Charlie had been killed and Frankie knew all about it.

The family held a funeral service at the local church and buried the skull and a few more bones that they had found in the hollow tree. The sheriff went back to his office and made up the papers to arrest Frankie and any family members that helped her. He found from some neighbors that Frankie's father and older brother had been hunting with them until the day before Christmas so he knew they were not involved. He couldn't figure how Frankie could have killed a grown man and chopped him up by herself so he decided to arrest Frankie, her mother and her younger brother. He took them to Morganton because at that time the whole western territory in North Carolina was in Burke County and Morganton was the county seat. And that is where they had her trial.

Frankie would not tell her story to anyone other than her own family. And after much discussion the sheriff decided he didn't have enough evidence to hold the mother and the brother so he let them go. Frankie stayed in jail for a long time while the sheriff interrogated family and neighbors, trying to piece together what had happened. In the meantime, some of the ladies in Morganton took pity on Frankie and started visiting her regularly and bringing her food. Finally after gaining Frankie's trust, Frankie did tell her story to a prominent lady in town and she wrote it down. Later, though, after Frankie was found guilty she asked the lady to destroy the notes because of the involvement of her brother and mother so the lady did.

Frankie was in jail for several years before the trial was over. At one point when it looked doubtful that she would get free the father bribed the jailer and helped Frankie escape from jail. They cut off her hair and dressed her as a man and headed west but the rains had been heavy that spring. The roaring river prevented them from crossing and the sheriff caught up with them and recognized Frankie. He took her back to Morganton and the trial was continued.

Frankie was found guilty and sentenced to die by hanging. For almost a year there were appeals and even petitions were signed but the governor refused to budge on the case. It was probably the awful way that Frankie and her family had disposed of Charlie's body.

Charlie's family eventually found other parts of Charlie's body. The lights were hidden under a rock and other parts were found in a shallow grave that Frankie's brother had managed to dig a little in the frozen ground. Charlie has three small graves up on the hill in the churchyard at the Baptist Church.

Frankie was hung in Morganton in July of 1838. Her father got her body and headed home with it but it was so hot that day. The body began to stink, so they set out to find a burying spot near Morganton. They dug several false graves because back then medical students from Raleigh were allowed to have a convicted murderer's body to experiment with so her father was afraid they would look for it. He finally found a final resting place in some unclaimed woods in Morganton and buried her there and only family members knew that location. They were known to visit it on occasion to put flowers there. Little Nancy was raised by her mother's family and moved away to another county.

"And that is the story of our Frankie as told to me by her brother." The Grandfather gave a sigh and looked out of the window. The snow had stopped and the sun had started setting behind the mountains over on the ridge where Frankie and Charlie's cabin use to be.

When the Grandfather looked down at his grandsons he saw that his audience had grown, Lila Ann had joined them and so had Willie who had found a seat in a nearby chair.

"Well, that explains that horrible night I and my friends spent in a tree. We never heard such screaming. Pa insists that it was a panther caught in a trap up over that ridge. I just don't know but we never will go hunting over there again."

"Is that enough for your story, Joe Henry?" the Grandfather asked.

"Can I write about it too?" Nathan interrupted.

"No, you can't!" Joe Henry exclaimed as his nostrils flared, "It is my idea to use that story. Go find your own story."

"I'll tell you what Nathan, tomorrow after supper I'll tell you the story of how I came to this country from my native country, France. That should make an interesting tale for you to write about."

"Oh yes, grandfather, did you see any ghosts in your story?" The Grandfather chuckled as Ora entered the parlor to announce supper was ready.

CHAPTER 9
THE TRIP FROM FRANCE

The next day the Grandfather returned to the parlor to wait for the cousins to come home from school. The cold day dawned with snow still on the ground from the day before. The Grandfather had retrieved his organ grinder from his room so he could include it in with the story he planned to tell Nathan for his Folk Tale homework. He was surprised by the larger audience, which had grown again to include some of the friends of the cousins. Mary had gotten permission to come home with Lila Ann and Joe Henry had brought one of his friends, Todd, home too.

"Grandfather, we told our friends about your story and they wondered if you would mind if they stayed to hear,"

Nathan asked since he was the one the story was for anyway.

"No, I don't mind at all," the Grandfather smiled, "Come sit here around me so you can hear better what I have to say.

Nathan frowned and made one comment, "I didn't like what Andy Cox said about you today at recess time when we were talking about you."

"What did he have to say, Nathan?" the Grandfather raised his bushy gray eyebrows.

"He said his father, Zeb told at the store one day that you came to hide out here in these mountains because you got in trouble with the law down in Florida. He said you married Grandma Claudine so her father would give you land."

Joe Henry spoke up, "Yeah, I wanted to punch his smart mouth! Mary and Lila Ann wouldn't let me."

"You've been in enough trouble after that fight with Tommy Stewart. I don't know if Mr. Wills would have understood again," Mary said as she smiled at Joe Henry. And her comment was all it took to calm Joe Henry down. She had a magic hold on him at this point in his life.

The Grandfather chuckled, "Joe Henry, you can't go fighting everyone who doesn't agree with you. You'll never grow up to be an adult. Let me get my story started so our guests can get home before dark. When I was a young man of fifteen in France........ "

My mother had just passed away leaving me an orphan. My father had died the year before and I was an only child. My mother tried to take care of us by working in a hospital in Lyon, France. Lyon is a very old town near the Alps, which are very high mountains in Europe. I worked for a while helping in the hospital where my mother had worked when I met a wealthy American who asked me if I would like to come to America.

When this man got out of the hospital, he arranged for me to work for my passage to America on a transport ship to Natchez, Mississippi. It took months to come to America on that ship, and I had to work very hard. I didn't mind, though. It was a wonderful adventure for a young man. When we docked in the port at Natchez, I found out that there was a deadly outbreak of the disease of cholera in the town.

This is the disease that had killed my mother, so I decided to head east toward Florida. I worked my way there, and I was very careful of the water that I drank. It was so hard to find good water. This country was wild and wooly and I had many adventures but I seemed to be always thirsty. I spent several years in Florida working at odd jobs. One night I decided to set in on a poker game one of the men that I worked with had gone to play. I was very lucky that night. One man who owed me money confessed to me he didn't have enough to pay me so he offered me his prized possession, his monkey and an organ grinder.

Now, in France I had seen many shows that the gypsies put on with live animals and music such as this so I took him up on his offer. I decided I would make some money for myself and put together a little act with music and the little monkey. Oh, she and I became good friends and she lived longer than most monkeys do because I took good care of her. People laughed and laughed at my little Babbette's antics.

Soon I grew tired of the hot climate and I decided to take the monkey and find a more comfortable place to live. I also found that people grew bored with the monkey and me after a while, so we took our show on the road. I traveled up the coast and enjoyed the many towns that I stayed in and entertained with my monkey. Her antics in our act kept us from starving. I especially liked Charleston on the coast of South Carolina. The people were gracious there and I stayed there longer than I did some of the other cities. I spent many months there with the monkey but eventually the heat of the summer got to me and I chose to move on north.

While I was in Charleston I met a man from the mountains who was there on business. He sang the praises of the beauty of his home and of the breathtaking scenery. The one thing he spoke of that really got my attention was the clear mountain springs and the plentiful water. I set my sights on coming to the mountains. I met up with a man in North Carolina who was headed for the Western Mountains so we came with him to Asheville.

Asheville was a rough little town before the Civil War and I took my little Babbette and headed to where there weren't as many people. When I came here I met your great-grandfather and went to work for him. Claudine's father was a very gracious man who had a large farm and blacksmith shop. Everyone that came to the shop enjoyed the monkey especially his daughter, Claudine. I use to tease your grandmother. I told her that she fell in love with my little monkey and just married me so she could have the monkey.

We built a little cabin, which is the original part of the cabin that Lila Ann had been living in since she was born. Later after we started our family we built this fine farmhouse we are in now. Claudine made Babbette wear a diaper when she was in our cabin. In fact, she treated Babbette like she was a baby. Babbette died the first winter we were married. I guess the cold in these mountains was just too much for the little monkey. And I wasn't really sure how old Babbette was, either. We buried her up in the family cemetery. Claudine painted the headstone that is on the monkey's grave.

Claudine cried and cried when that monkey died. I was very glad when she found out that she was pregnant with your Uncle Robert. Robert was born in the cabin. Lafayette came along later and he was born here in this house right after we moved into it.

Ten years ago when Claudine died I didn't think I could stand it. And that winter after she died I thought the cold and snow would chill me to my bones. Robert talked me into coming to the Piedmont where it is a little warmer in the winter. When I thought that I was dying I just wanted to be here near Claudine and these beautiful mountains, home.

"Wow, grandfather, I'm glad you aren't dying. Are you going to stay here with us now or go back to live with Uncle Robert?" Joe Henry asked.

"If your father doesn't mind, I would love to stay here," the Grandfather smiled.

Fate had been standing near the door and heard the last part of his father's story and he commented, "I should say we need you! Who else could tell stories better than you? Except for maybe Joe Henry, I think he needs to learn how to play that organ grinder too."

"And I can be the monkey!" Nathan exclaimed and jumped up and started dancing around the room.

Joe Herny looked up at the Grandfather and asked, "The next time you tell us a story can it be about the gypsies in France?"

"Oui, I can tell many stories about them. I've heard they originally came to Europe from India. We can save that for next time."

Ora appeared at the door, "Supper is ready and our guests can eat with us too and Willie will take them home in the wagon."

CHAPTER 10
THE TRIP TO VIRGINIA

The next week at school turned out to be a very busy one. Mr. Wills didn't require students to read their stories but some wanted to do it anyway. Joe Henry and Nathan read their stories and everyone wanted to hear them. The class sat very still as Joe Henry read his paper on the story of Frankie. And the story Nathan wrote about the Grandfather and the monkey and organ grinder made the students just as still. Lila Ann decided to write about Rose's wedding but she chose not to read it aloud because of her shyness so Mr. Wills read it to the class. All three cousins received an A for their grades.

"Mary your story sounds wonderful! Please do read it," Lila Ann begged, "Or ask Mr. Wills to read it."

"It will only bring laughter to the other children, Lila Ann. And I don't want to be laughed at," Mary said with a tear in her eye.

"May I see your story, Mary?" Mr. Wills said standing over the two girls without either realizing it until he spoke. "What is the story about?"

"It is about the Yunwi Tsundi, the Tricksters, who were our Little People. They are like your Irish Leprechauns. The Cherokee have many stories about them. The stories have been handed down from generation to generation in my family," Mary said as she gently handed her teacher her papers.

"Thank you for allowing me to read this story to the class, Mary. It sounds like a wonderful story and I, for one, am very excited about this. Since the day has gone so quickly by and it is time to go home, I will read this first thing in the morning. Class dismissed."

The next morning, school started with an air of excitement. Mary Maney was the last one in her seat. Mr. Wills almost began to worry when he came into the class with Mary's seat empty.

"Good morning, class."

"Good morning, Mr. Wills," the class said in unison.

"I read over your story last night, Mary. And I want to assure you that it is another A paper. It is an excellent story as well and I want to thank you for sharing it with us and choosing this subject to write about." With that said, Mr. Wills began to read.

One winter a small Cherokee family that lived in a rented cabin began the day with their breakfast of com mush and water from the nearby spring. It had been a very harsh winter so far especially on the father who had to work outside for the railroad. It had snowed for several days and the father, mother, and tiny daughter had eaten almost all of the food they had stored up in the summer months.

Finally the snow stopped and the father and mother decided to dress themselves and their tiny daughter up very warmly and head out into the forest to find some food. They walked for several hours and found nothing but snow. They came to a rocky area in the woods and, being very tired, decided to stop and rest. The mother sat her tiny daughter down on a large boulder to rest her arms from carrying her daughter. The father thought he heard a noise and said that it might be an animal caught in a trap. If it is an animal caught in a trap then they could borrow it to fix for food. The father reasoned that later when the snow was gone he could hunt for another animal to replace the one that they borrowed. The mother went with him thinking he might need help. Their tiny daughter they left resting on the boulder and they thought she would be fine until they returned.

When the young couple returned only a few minutes later with a small rabbit that had been killed in the trap they found their tiny daughter gone. There were many little footprints in the snow but they could not tell in which direction their daughter had gone because there were no footprints away from the large boulder but theirs.

They called and searched until they were very cold and tired, and it had grown dark. The father told the mother that they would go back to the cabin and cook the rabbit. The food would give them strength to start the search again first thing in the morning.

The next morning the young couple returned to the large boulder and began their search again. They searched for many days and found no trace of their tiny daughter. Every evening they would return home and cry themselves to sleep because they feared a wild animal had gotten their sweet tiny daughter and eaten her.

Finally the snow melted enough for the father to return to his job. Every day, the mother continued to go out and search until dark. When the father told his boss and the people that he worked with about his daughter's disappearance, they too came to help search for the little girl. They also found no trace of the little girl. The mother grew sadder and sadder and eventually went to bed with a strange illness.

Spring came and the flowers started blooming. The father decided to go out into the forest to pick some wild flowers to cheer his wife up and help to make her feel better. He went from one flower patch to another until he came to the boulder where they had been in the snow when they were looking for food. The father found the most beautiful flowers of all around the boulder. He bent over to pick the flowers there when he heard giggling nearby. The giggle sounded just like his tiny daughter's giggle he missed so much.

When the father looked up, there on the boulder sat his tiny daughter. Her winter wrappings were folded neatly next to her on the rock. Her face shined and her cheeks were so rosy and she looked plump and very healthy. The father cried out happily and picked her up hugging her tightly. That is when he saw them, the Little People, scurrying back under the boulder. They waved at him and disappeared.

Still hugging his daughter he ran as fast as he could run back to the cabin. He had given the beautiful flowers to his tiny daughter as he ran. What a sweet bouquet his wife received! When he got back with his present his wife cried out happily as well! She asked who had had their precious little daughter. She wanted to thank them for taking such good care of her. He told her the truth and warned her not to tell anyone because if you tell where to find the Little People and where they live, you will surely die.

"Wow!" Nathan exclaimed, "Is that story true, Mary?"

"It is one of many that were told to me by my grandmother about the Yunwi Tsundi, the Little People," Mary said and blushed a little.

"I do appreciate all of you," Mr. Wills said, "Everyone did an excellent job on this project. Thank you. Now, we will finish the day with our regular lessons on grade level. But before we get to that I understand that tomorrow morning Lila Ann and Anna Jane will be leaving to take a trip. We will miss you both. After lunch, we will have a little goodbye party for them before we dismiss for the weekend."

The North Carolina Mountains had seen no more snow just a couple of cold rains in November. The Ireland family prepared to leave for Virginia on a cool but sunny Saturday. Lockie said she felt strong enough to travel. Lila Ann had mixed emotions about leaving the only home she had ever known. Mr. Wills had helped find some information about Virginia for her and so had Rose's husband, Tom. Tom worked at the small college near Asheville and was studying to be a teacher too, so he had access to many books.

Lila Ann also dreaded leaving her cousins and the Grandfather with all of his stories. She could just sit for hours and listen to his French accent. Anna Jane, on the other hand didn't seem to mind, she got so excited about seeing her Pappy again.

"Have you got everything?" Ora asked as Lockie handed the baby to Lila Ann and climbed into the wagon.

"I think so," Lockie said taking the baby back from Lila Ann and adjusting herself on the buckboard seat.

Lila Ann looked around the wagon and did not see little Jimmy, "Mommy, I think there is one person we have overlooked."

Lockie turned and saw Anna Jane and Lila Ann sitting in the back of the wagon and realized that her little two-year-old son was not there. As she turned back around she exclaimed, "Oh my gosh, Jimmy!"

Willie walked out of the house holding Jimmy with one hand and Jesse with the other and said, "Are you missing someone? You know you never see one of these little guys without the other. I'm afraid these cousins are going to miss each other a lot."

Willie lifted Jimmy up into the wagon to his mother and then climbed up in the driver's seat. Both little cousins started to cry. Ora picked Jesse up to comfort him and said, "I guess you'll just have to leave Jimmy here with me. These two little boys have become very close to each other. Jesse will be lost without Jimmy."

"I know I'm going to miss everyone," Lockie sighed, "Someday, maybe, things will die down about that cabin burning and Charles and I can bring the young'uns back home."

"I sure hope so," Ora had tears in her eyes as she spoke.

"Wait, don't leave until I kiss my little petit mademoiselles goodbye!" the Grandfather said as he came from around the side of the house. "I will miss all of the cousins and Lockie too!" he added.

Lila Ann hugged the Grandfather's neck and whispered in his ear, "I will miss you, my Grandfather, and the stories you tell. Please don't die until we can move back home."

"I will do my very best not to die, Lila Ann," the Grandfather looked to the edge of the clearing and noted, "I think you have someone else here to say goodbye to you. It is Mary Maney."

Mary stood just at the edge of the clearing with her father, Ed. As they walked closer Mary said, "We wanted to bring you something to take with you on your journey, Lila Ann. I made it especially for you."

Mary and her father walked over to the wagon. Mary handed Lila Ann a small black vase with a very fancy design scratched into it. "This vase has an old Cherokee pattern on it. The pattern is called the friendship pattern. I wanted you to have something that I have made with my own hands."

Lockie looked at the vase and said, "This is very beautiful, Mary. Tell me how do you get the pot so black and shiny?"

"I rub the coil pot with a river rock that my grandmother gave me after the pot is dried in the air. Then I bum it in a pit in the ground using only pinewood. And when the ashes cool you have a shiny, black pot. I used a sharp stick to make the design while the clay was still wet. My grandmother uses paddles with carved designs in them. She would hit the clay hard with the paddle while the clay is still wet to make a design that has been carved into the wood paddle. Grandmother always teased me and said she would paddle me with the bigger paddles if I misbehaved."

Joe Henry, Nathan, and Fate came out of the barn. Joe Henry said, "Mary, when did you get here?"

Joe Henry ran ahead of his father and brother, "Look at that beautiful vase! Did you make that, Mary? Say, when are you going to show me how to make pottery like that?"

"Maybe I will teach you sometime when you aren't busy hunting or playing ball or something," Mary smiled.

"Well, we'd better be getting along. You have a train to catch in Erwin," Willie said as he picked up the reins and the mules shuffled along. They were ready to move too.

"Thank you very much, Mary. I am really going to miss you! Maybe you can come to visit me in the summer," Lila Ann fought back the tears as the wagon pulled out and she waved goodbye to her friends and family.

The trip over the mountains was a quiet one except for the rattle of the wagon and the clopping of the mules. The baby cried a couple of times and they stopped to use the bathroom in the laurel thicket several times. Jimmy fell off to sleep after a small crying spell. Lila Ann cried softly to herself some too. And Anna Jane all bright-eyed thought the trip was a great adventure. The family arrived in Erwin alert and eager. Even the ones who were sad suddenly realized that they were on an adventure and would soon see their Pappy. The Ireland cousins had never been more than twenty miles from their mountain home.

Because there had been no rain in Erwin for several weeks the street in Erwin blew dust on them so much it caused the family to cough. They got quickly across the street to the railroad station. Their first time on a train became very real to them. When they heard the whistle blow, Lockie turned to give them instructions, "Now, stay close to me all of you and Lila Ann hold both Anna Jane and Jimmy's hands cause I have the baby to hold. Willie will see to our bags."

Willie did just that after he secured the mules. Lockie went into the station to buy their tickets. Lila Ann followed with Anna Jane and Jimmy in tow. Lila Ann had never seen such a world as this one. It excited her just watching all of the wagons and horses and the people milling about. She had watched the trains many times going down the tracks in the mountains but when she heard the engine outside, she had to drag Anna Jane and Jimmy over to see it.

"Look at these dirty, dusty windows," Lockie observed as the children watched the train arriving. "Who takes care of the station? They need to clean these windows."

The children were so mesmerized by the trains they didn't even hear their mother's concern over the windows.

They all stood with noses pressed against the window until Lockie walked over and pulled them away.

Willie walked over and gave his Aunt Lockie a hug and said, "I hope your trip is a safe one. Let us know when you get there. Mama will be beside herself until she hears from you." He reached down and rubbed each head of his cousins and then turned and kissed the baby on the head.

"Thank you, Willie. Let us know when that girl says yes," Lockie chuckled, "and thank you for all the help that you have given us." She gave him another hug and said, "Be careful on the ride home, goodbye." They all turned to wave at Willie, even little Jimmy.

"All right, it is time to board the train," Lockie said and place the baby on her shoulder so she could help the children get up the stairs to the door of the train as a gentleman inside the train who saw the little family and stepped over to help them.

"Thank you so much," Lockie said to the man.

"You are quite welcome," the gentleman said and returned to his seat.

This was the second time Lockie had been on a train and she felt as giddy as her children. She looked down at them all as they settled themselves into their seats. She was glad the tears over leaving their home had stopped. And she found herself thinking of seeing her husband again. She remembered the first time she rode a train, with

Charles on a short trip to Asheville before she had Lila Ann.

When the train pulled out with a jerk, Jimmy started to cry. Lockie handed the baby to Lila Ann so she could pick him up and comfort him. She brought his attention to the town that had started moving outside their window. After Jimmy got quiet she sat him on the seat next to her and placed him so he could see out the train window. Lockie then took the baby back from Lila Ann.

"You can get close to the window now to see what is passing by," Lockie said and smiled at Lila Ann. "Lila Ann, you have grown so much and you are such a big help to me. I just don't know what I'd do without you." Lila Ann turned and smiled back at her mother and quickly turned back to watch out the window.

Lila Ann started thinking about the first letter she would write to Joe Henry and Nathan about this trip. She knew neither one of her cousins had been on a train and she couldn't wait to write them about it. Lockie sat watching her children, and she too noticed the scenery rushing by, especially the mountains. They loomed behind them like a high uneven wall. The colors of fall had gone and they looked blue and gray. She also realized she had spent most of her life there in the safety of that wall. She suddenly felt exposed and unprotected. As the train chugged on away from the mountains that she dearly loved, a tear ran down Lockie' s cheek.

CHAPTER 11
NEW HOME IN VIRGINIA

After several hours of travel through the hills of Tennessee, the little family finally reached their destination of Damascus, Virginia, just across the Tennessee State line. Damascus had only a small train depot that sat at the edge of a sleepy little town unlike the town of Erwin. As they pulled into the station Anna Jane first spotted her father standing next to a wagon just behind the railroad station.

"Look, there is Pappy!" she cried.

Lockie needed relief and she knew she would get it when they arrived at their new home and got out of her restricting clothes. She needed to feed Aaron and her dress didn't allow the feeding of a baby, which she wouldn't have done in public anyway. Without being told, Lila Ann got Anna Jane and Jimmy by the hand and led them toward the exit, Lockie following with baby Aaron.

"I'm so glad to see you and I'm glad that the train got in on time!" Lockie said as Charles grabbed both her and the baby. The baby who slept soundly in her arms woke up and started to cry. Before Charles could move, the other three children had him around the legs.

"Whoa, there," Charles said as he reached down and gathered up his children releasing Lockie so she could calm down the crying baby.

"Let me get your bags loaded and we can be off and headed to our new home," Charles said and turned to go to the back of the train. Lockie handed Lila Ann the baby as she helped Anna Jane and Jimmy get into the wagon. Charles came up from behind and placed the bags in the wagon and helped Lockie up onto the front buckboard seat. He then lifted Lila Ann with the baby into the wagon. He jumped into the driver's seat and grabbed the reins.

"My boss let me use the company wagon to come meet you," Charles smiled over at Lockie who now had little Aaron cuddled close to her. He fretted a little because he was tired and hungry. Lila Ann looked around as they rode out of town. She noticed that there weren't as many people here as there had been in Erwin. She also wondered if she could ever be happy in this strange new place. It began to get dark as they pulled up to their new home. The house, still visible in the fading evening light, looked inviting to the little family just because it was the first time that they were together in a long time.

"It is a cute little white frame house with a nice front porch," Lila Ann commented. She looked around and noticed the street of houses and they all looked just like their house. Then she had a strange thought; what if she came home one day and went to the wrong house? How she wished this were all a dream and she would wake up in her own cabin in the mountains. She didn't say anything, though; she just looked up at her Pappy and smiled. And that is when she noticed he had been studying her.

"Are you all right, Lila Ann?" Charles asked.

"Yes, Pappy, I'm fine," She looked away and added, "Just a little tired."

"Lila Ann, sweetie, can you help me with your little brothers while you're Pappy and I unload the wagon?" Lockie interrupted her thoughts.

"Yes'um."

The next day after a good night's sleep the little family got up for a Sunday morning breakfast. The church bell rang down the road.

Charles walked out on the tiny back porch that was off of the kitchen and Lockie joined him holding little Aaron. Charles reached for the baby and said, "Working for the lumber mill isn't so bad. The boss has been very nice to me. This reminds me, I have to take his wagon back today. And tomorrow we'll take the girls to school down by the

Douglas Trestle. They have a three-room schoolhouse here. I met the principal on Friday. His name is Bill Shearer. He also teaches high school there and there are two other teachers."

"Pappy, do I have to go tomorrow? Can't I stay and help Mommy unpack?" Lila Ann asked.

Charles stopped and looked at his oldest child and asked, "Are you afraid to go to the new school?"

"Yes Pappy, I am. I miss Joe Henry and Nathan and my best friend, Mary," She said with a tear in her eye.

"Now, Lila Ann you get along so good with people. Why, it won't take you any time to make new friends!" Charles tousled her hair.

The next morning during breakfast Lila Ann sat sullen and quiet. While Anna Jane was bubbling over, "Mommy, are there many children in the new school? Are you going with us?"

"No dear, I have to stay home with Jimmy and Aaron. Your Pappy is taking you to school. It isn't that far to walk. It is only two streets over. Pappy will show you both where it is and tomorrow you can walk all by yourself."

Charles came in the back door. He had clean clothes on and he wasn't wearing his overalls. Lila Ann looked up at him through her eyelashes. The only time she had ever seen him dress like that was when he got dressed up for church or to go to a funeral or a wedding. He looked so different somehow. And she wondered would her life ever be the same?

"All right, girls, are we ready?"

"Yes, Pappy!" Anna Jane bubbled again.

This is the first time Lila Ann ever wanted to wipe the silly smile off of her sister's face. How could Anna Jane be so excited when she felt so afraid? As they walked out the door Charles noticed the difference in his two daughters. Anna Jane almost skipped down the street and Lila Ann just plotted along. He slowed down to walk beside her so they could talk.

"I know change is hard as you get older, Lila Ann. Don't resent Anna Jane's enthusiasm or hate her for it. She's only to school for a couple of months and she has an older sister to protect her and you don't. I know you really miss Joe Henry and Nathan, cause they looked out for you. Life is full of changes. This won't be the last new thing you'll have to deal with in your life. Do the best that you can. Listen a lot and watch people, study them. You'll learn a lot about what people here will expect from you if you just observe them."

A month later while sitting in her class in school, Lila Ann remembered the words her father had told her that first day of school. She had made several friends, but no one could take Mary's place. Mary was different and very special and Lila Ann realized that now even more. Sometimes she missed home so bad it physically hurt but she never shared that with anyone not even her parents.

She poured her heart out to her friend Mary in letters. Mary wrote back, but she and Joe Henry had a full-fledged romance going on, so she had someone. Lila Ann had made a few friends but, mostly she stayed to herself.

"Lila Ann, I'm walking home with Susan. Will you tell Mommy I'll be home in about an hour to do my chores, please?" Anna Jane had sure adjusted better than Lila Ann had. Anna Jane had several friends but Susan Hobbs was her favorite new friend. Susan was six years old too and only child. Lila Ann had tried very hard to do what her father had told her when it came to her sister. Anna Jane's success at school and making friends so easily only made Lila Ann feel more lost and alone.

"Lila Ann, wake up child! What did you do with your homework papers? I didn't receive them with the others on my desk this morning." Mabel Rhodes said as she stood over Lila Ann's desk. She taught the middle grades at Lila Ann's new school. Lockie called her an old maid schoolteacher. She had taken a liking to Lila Ann and knew that she was not a happy child.

"I'm sorry, Miss Rhodes, I forgot to put them in my book this morning. I did do my homework, honest," Lila Ann said as she yawned, "I did not sleep good last night so I just stayed up and finished my homework and read." She had also gotten so busy in the morning with getting a letter to Mary ready to mail that she forgot her homework papers altogether.

"All right, my child, I will take points off of it for being late, and stay after school, I want to talk to you."

"Yes'um," Lila Ann said and hung her head down. Now she was in trouble. Somehow, though, she really didn't care.

After school Lila Ann came up to Miss Rhodes' s desk and stood quietly waiting for the punishment she knew had to come. She had resigned herself to take it and go on home.

"Lila Ann, thank you for not forgetting to stay after school. Some children would have run off when I ask them to have a conference with me after school," Mabel Rhodes said with a big smile, "I want to speak with your parents about your progress in school. Will you please see that they get my note?" She handed a sealed envelope to Lila Ann.

"Yes'um," was all that Lila Ann replied as she slowly turned and walked out the door. As she walked toward the little white frame house small delicate snowflakes started falling all around her. She thought about her cabin in the mountains and how beautiful the snow was there and how much she longed to be there. Joe Henry would be getting out the sled and he and Nathan would let her and Anna Jane ride down the hill beside the barn with them. They always had so much fun in the winter!

When Lila Ann got home she went straight to find her mother. Lockie sat at the table in front of the cook stove with a pot of potatoes peeling them for supper while her two little boys played on a blanket in the floor.

"Oh, is school out already?" Lockie said and got up to throw the potato peelings away. "Where is Anna Jane?"

"Anna Jane walked home with Susan again to see if she could come over here to play before supper," Lila Ann replied as she handed her mother the sealed envelope from Miss Rhodes.

"What is this?"

"It is a note from Miss Rhodes."

"Is something wrong?" Lockie said as she opened the envelope.

"I forgot my homework at home this morning," Lila Ann said and sat on the blanket to play with Aaron and Jimmy. The baby loved his sisters and always giggled and laughed when they paid any attention to him.

Lockie read the letter that Mabel Rhodes had written and it was more about her concern for Lila Ann than any homework. Mabel discussed how Lila Ann seemed so distant and frequently fell asleep in class. She was concerned that she preferred to stay to herself and had difficulty working with other students.

Lockie sat down in the chair and watched Lila Ann play with the boys. She and Charles had both noticed Lila Ann's despondency. They had wondered too why she had not made new friends at school. Lockie just didn't know the answer. It was only a week until Christmas and they would be having the Christmas play next week at school. She would talk to her teacher then about this problem.

Maybe after the holidays Lila Ann would perk up but in Lockie's heart she knew that probably wouldn't happen. With all the money that Charles was making now they were going to have the best Christmas they had ever had. Surely that would help Lila Ann to feel better.

Christmas came and went. Everyone in the Ireland family seemed to just enjoy each other and Christmas so much. Lila Ann tried really hard to pretend she was happier. She even started spending more time with Stephanie, her new friend from across the street. Stephanie had three older brothers and her father also worked at the lumberyard, as did most of the families living in her neighborhood.

Miss Rhodes and Lila Ann's parents had a long discussion about her at the Christmas play and had exchanged several notes after Christmas about her. They agreed to encourage her to make friends her own age and give her more time to adjust. Lila Ann learned to hide her feelings and keep her longings for the mountain home to herself. During this time she became interested in drawing and would spend hours drawing pictures of the cabin and the things she remembered from home. The months turned into a year and things at the lumberyard began to slow down. A war was coming and the discussion of it spread from town to her classroom even to home. The place that this war would happen would be across the ocean in Europe.

"I think we are going to move back to Tennessee," Charles announced one evening after coming in late for supper from the lumberyard. "Things just aren't going well at work and I'm tired of all of the competition between the other workers that are afraid of being laid off."

"Oh Charles, can we go back home? Do you think it would be safe?" Lockie looked up from her mending.

"Get a letter off to your sister's family. See what Fate can find out about a job over around Erwin."

Lila Ann stood just inside the kitchen door when she heard her father say write home to her cousins. She jumped into the room and said, "Mommy, are we going to move back home?"

"Maybe to Erwin, Tennessee, I don't know. I need to write to Fate and Ora and see what is going on there."

CHAPTER 12
THE LETTER

The mail delivery came before Lockie could finish her own letter to her sister. Charles came running into the house waving the letter from home. "I've got a letter here from Fate. I'm too excited to read it. Here, Lockie read it to me!"

Lockie pulled out the letter with difficulty. She was excited too. She hadn't heard from Ora since her Christmas card and letter. She knew that Rose and Tom were expecting a baby in the summer and Willie hadn't proposed yet to Cindy. She sure hoped that everyone was all right. It was very unusual for Fate to write a letter.

"I hope John is all right," Lockie worried out loud and finally got the letter out and unfolded.

"Charles," she read, "I hope this letter gets to you before I do. We've had a big snow here so I haven't been able to ride to get you. Ora has been sick but she is on the mend so tell Lockie not to fret none. I am writing to tell you about Zeb Cox. Last week some rough outliers waited on Zeb to be left alone in the store around dark. Zeb's older son, Jonathan was gone to Asheville and Zeb's wife has had the flu. She isn't doing very well. Anyway, those outliers robbed Zeb and beat him nearly to death! The sheriff has a posse out after them. Jonathan came to the house last night and asked me if I knew how to get in touch with you. He promised me this was not a trick but I went to see Zeb for myself. They don't expect him to live. He looked pretty bad, Charles. Anyway, he asked me to get in touch with you. He wants to see you before he dies. I didn't know what to tell him. I told him that I would write to you. He wouldn't tell me what he wanted. He said he needed to tell you something and he wanted to tell you to your face. I'll leave it up to you. I don't think he will last much longer than a week. If you can get the train to Erwin, I will pick you up at the train station just let me know when or if you are coming and don't take too long because Zeb is not long for this world. Sincerely, your brother-in-law, Fate Laboree." Lockie finished and looked up at Charles.

"I'll pack a few things and go talk to my boss. You'll be all right if I'm gone a few days. I have to find out what he wants. Fate saw him and how bad off he is. I don't think he is setting a trap for me."

Charles walked over and looked into the living room at Lila Ann playing with her two little brothers on a blanket on the floor. Charles turned to Lockie and said, "Lila Ann is grieving herself to death. She hasn't said anything since before our first Christmas here but I can see it in her eyes."

Lockie got up to look into the living room at the children and said, "We'll be fine. You just be very careful and come back soon and let me know how Ora is doing. Maybe she'll need some help."

"Don't let Lila Ann know that I'm going home. I don't want to get her hopes up. She was happy just at the possibility of moving to Erwin, Tennessee. We can leave it at that for now."

Charles was able to get the train to Erwin early the next morning. Lockie was more worried than she let on. What if Zeb really thought that Charles set that cabin fire? He could be setting a trap even on his deathbed. She knew she had to be strong and not let on to her children. Charles sent the wire from the train station as soon as he found out the approximate time of arrival in Erwin. Even though he enjoyed the money he had been making at the lumberyard, he was very excited at the possibility of going home. The question ran through his head again and again on the trip, what on earth did Zeb Cox want so desperately to tell him?

Lila Ann and Anna Jane went to school that day and Lila Ann was in an unusually good mood. The thought of moving even to Erwin and closer to the mountains had filled her with hope. Anna Jane liked her new home and she wasn't too happy about the idea of leaving her new friends, but as long as she was with her father, she would be happy anywhere. That afternoon the girls walked home together.

"Lila Ann are you happy about leaving Virginia?" Anna Jane asked.

"Yes, Anna Jane but I'd be happier if we were moving back home to our cabin."

Anna Jane thought for a minute then said, "I miss Joe Henry and Nathan and the stories the Grandfather told. I miss the fun we had in the snow. Where is Erwin, Tennessee?"

"It is right next to our mountains," Lila Ann said with a laugh, and it was the first time she had laughed in a year.

About the time the girls were arriving home from school, Charles arrived at the train station in Erwin. Fate had gotten his wire by a messenger from Cox's store. Jonathan had to mind the store now that his dad was so sick and his mother was still not completely well from the flu.

Fate had rode horseback and brought another horse along for Charles to ride. It would be a much faster trip over the mountain on horseback.

"Jonathan's note said that his father was not doing well and that he would probably close the store early so he can go home. He also said he would tell his father that you are on your way," Fate explained as they rode toward the North Carolina Mountains.

A cold light snow blew over them and there still remained snow on the ground from several days before, but it wasn't bad enough to cause any problems on the trip home. As they rode into the steep mountain pass Charles realized how much he really missed his home. He thought about Lila Ann and how much these mountains meant to her. She would be so happy if they could all come home. Maybe this meeting with Zeb Cox would help make that possible. They didn't stop at the Laboree farm because it would be out of the way to go there and it would soon be dark.

They finally arrived at the Cox's big three story white frame house. It sat at the end of a tree lined street on the edge of a small mountain town on the French Broad River just north of Asheville. They were one of the very few people in the mountains that actually had servants to help with the cleaning and care of the property. Zeb Cox had done very well with his store and farm. One of the hired men met them and took their horses to see to their care after the hard ride from Tennessee. Jonathan met them on the porch. He had just had time to close the store and arrive home to get his father ready for their visit.

"Thank you for coming, Charles. My father could not rest until he saw you. And thank you, Fate for getting him here," Jonathan said and extended his hand first to Charles, then to Fate, as he turned to lead them into the house.

"Please forgive my mother for not greeting you herself. We almost lost her to the flu but she is recovering, just still very weak and is in bed resting. The doctor said there have been several deaths in the community from the flu. We are very lucky to still have my mother with us."

Jonathan led them up the stairs to his father's room. Charles looked inquisitively at Jonathan as he opened the bedroom door for them. Jonathan caught Charles's look and said, "My father will explain why he wanted to see you and I'll be right here to help him if he has any difficulty doing that."

Zeb's appearance had not improved since Fate last saw him; in fact, Fate thought he looked even worse. He had a dull gray color to his skin now. The bruises on his face were even worse and more visible now that some of the bandages had been removed. Fate sighed heavily when he saw Zeb.

"Papa, Charles and Fate are here. Charles has come a long way to see you," Jonathan bent down and whispered into his father's ear.

Zeb managed to open both eyes although his right eye didn't open all of the way because of the bad bruise on it. It took some effort but Zeb attempted to talk, "Charles, Charles Ireland." His voice was barely above a whisper and Charles could see that he was very weak.

"Yes, I'm here," Charles answered and bent down low enough so that Zeb could see him better.

"Charles Ireland, I know you left your home and family because of me. I accused you of setting fire to my cabin. My son and the sheriff did not know that I had asked you to do it for $100. I believed every man had his price," Zeb said and started to cough. Jonathan stepped over to help his father sit up a little better in bed so that he would be more able to talk without coughing.

"I had just taken out new insurance on all of my property and I desperately needed money. It was the only way that I had to get a lot of money quickly," Zeb stopped and looked over at his son. Jonathan hung his head down as Zeb continued, "You see Jonathan had a problem with gambling and he had gotten himself into a bad situation that could have cost him his life."

Zeb reached for Charles's hand and said, "Charles, I was a desperate and proud man. My pride meant more to me than you or your family. I set that fire myself when I couldn't get you to do it. And I told the sheriff that you did it to get to sharecrop that land yourself so no one else would move into that cabin the McCall's had lived in."

Zeb started coughing again and Jonathan tried to help him move up on his pillow but Zeb refused to let go of Charles's hand as he continued, "I'm not finished."

"If you need my forgiveness, Zeb you have it!" Charles spoke up.

"Yes, I do, Charles but I also wanted to face you before I died and tell you how much I know I've made you and your family suffer. And I wanted to try and make it up to you somehow. I want you to have the property that surrounds that cabin of Fate's you and your family lived in. I also want you to have the land the McCall cabin use to set on. Jonathan will see to it and that you have the materials and workers to build your own home where you want to on that property." Zeb sighed heavily and lay back onto his pillow. It had taken all of his strength to tell Charles what he needed to tell him.

Jonathan took his father's hands and folded them on his chest and covered them. He turned to Charles and Fate and said, "I'll see to everything. All you have to do is see that your family gets back home safely. And, Charles, I'm truly sorry this happened. It is really all my fault and I will personally help you build your new home. I was young and wild and stupid. My father loved me and he would have done anything to protect me from myself."

He looked down at his father as he continued, "Now, Papa can rest. He hasn't slept since he first told me the whole story. I thought my father had all the money in the world, I never knew that I had run through about all of it with my foolishness. I've had to do some growing up fast. I was very lucky the insurance company didn't take us to court. I have made arrangements to repay them."

The two men said their goodbyes and wished Jonathan well for not only his father but his mother too. They headed for the Laboree farm. Charles was so excited. He looked toward Fate in the dark as they rode along at a slower pace than they had to get there and said, "I can't wait to get home and tell Lockie and the children! Lila Ann has never been happy away from these mountains and her cousins and friends."

Ora greeted her husband and brother-in-law at the door even though she was still feeling poorly, "What happened?" was all she could get out.

They sat at the kitchen table and told Ora the whole story over coffee. Charles made plans to bring his family home.

"You can move back into that cabin of the Grandfather's until you get your new house built," Fate offered. "Joe Henry, Nathan and I will move the furniture and cook stove back for you while you go back to Virginia to get Lockie and the kids. Willie can go with you and take the mules and wagon."

"Yes and when we all get back home we are going to have us one big barn raising wing ding!" Willie said from the back door where he had stood listening.

"Oui and we can celebrate me not dying too!" John Laboree said coming in from the parlor door.

Joe Henry and Nathan came in from behind the Grandfather leading little Jesse and added, "Are our cousins coming home?"

"Yes, they sure are just as soon as Willie and I can go get them!" Charles said.

Jesse added, "Oh boy, Jimmy comes home!"

"Yes, Jesse, your cousin Jimmy is coming home too," Fate said as he picked up his youngest son.

"We'll plan that wing ding for a spring barn raising! I'll get out my fiddle and Lockie can sing 'Little Mathey Groves,'"

"Boy, if Lockie sings that ballad we'll be up all night! That has got to be the longest ballad anyone ever sang," Charles laughed.

The next morning Charles got an early start. He took the mules and wagon to ride all the way to Virginia because they had acquired so many things since they left, it would have to be hauled in a wagon. Willie went with him to help. All the way to Virginia Willie talked about the war in Europe and how the United States would probably end up involved in it. Willie speculated that he would probably be drafted into the army.

CHAPTER 13
CAROLINA MOUNTAIN HOME

The morning after the Ireland family returned to the mountains, a messenger came to deliver a letter from Jonathan Cox. Fate answered the door and handed the letter to Charles as he came down the stairs to eat breakfast.

"It says that Zeb Cox passed away in his home last night. We are invited to the funeral the day after tomorrow at two o'clock at the Baptist Church. They will be receiving family and friends tomorrow evening at their home," Charles read and looked up at Fate, "It also said that Jonathan and his attorney request my presence at the reading of Zeb's will so that Jonathan can formally give me the title to the land and make arrangements to build my house."

Lila Ann and Lockie were standing on the stairs while Charles read the letter and Lockie said, "Then it is really true. Zeb gave you that land and Jonathan is really going to help build us a house? I was afraid you had imagined all of this or that I was dreaming." A tear rolled down her cheek.

Although Lila Ann said nothing the huge smile on her face and the once gone twinkle in her eye told Charles all he needed to know about his oldest. "Shall I get Anna Jane up to get ready to go to school?" Was all she said.

"Yes dear, why don't you do that?" Lockie hugged her and Lila Ann turned to go back up the stairs to wake Anna Jane.

"But don't wake Jimmy if you can help it. He is tired from the trip on that wagon. And if Anna Jane complains just let her sleep. Aren't you tired from the long trip too?"

"Oh no Mommy I want to see Mary so bad and walk to school again with Joe Henry and Nathan," Lila Ann said as she went on up the stairs.

A month passed and the Ireland family had settled back into their cabin. Construction on their new house had started and plans were being made for the spring barn raising and a big barn wing ding. John Laboree had shined up his organ grinder and Fate had tuned his fiddle. Ora felt a lot better and all excited about the new grand baby that was due at the end of July 1916.

The day of the barn raising arrived and eveiyone in the Ireland and Laboree household were up early. It was a beautiful spring Saturday morning. The sun had already peeked up over the mountain shooting its rays into the window of the kitchen in the little two-room cabin. Charles had been down to the site of the new house and was coming up through the back yard. With Aaron on her hip and Jimmy in his high chair, Lockie was practicing the ballads that she planned to sing that night at the wing ding, which would be held in their new barn next to the new house.

"Several of our neighbors are already down there. And Fate, Willie, Joe Henry, Nathan and Grandfather Laboree should be up here any minute," Charles said as he came in the back door. He had stopped to wash his hands on the back porch in the washbasin Lockie had placed out there for him. "It has been many years since we've had a real barn raising in this community."

"Your breakfast is ready and here is your coffee." Lockie handed him a steaming cup of coffee, "I can remember Granny talking about it when I was small, how the community would come together to help a new neighbor."

"Where are the girls?" Charles asked placing his coffee down but before Lockie could answer Charles reached for baby Aaron.

"They have been playing with the baby while I fixed breakfast," Lockie beamed at Charles as he played with Aaron now.

"We could hear your singing down at the new house. The men were commenting how good it was," Charles said handing her Aaron and kissing her on the cheek, "Are you going to sing 'Little Mathey Groves' tonight?"

"You know I always get requests for that one. Granny use to say that was one of them long-winded ballads and one of her favorite love songs. You know if I were Lord Daniel's wife in England, I wouldn't of lied to save my own life either."

"Who taught that love song to your Granny?"

"Why her mama, of course! I guess that song goes back several generations to whoever brought it over from England. I just hope one of my girls takes up singing so we can keep those old ballads a goin'."

The barn raising would be the first one in thirty years and in the new century. It would also be well attended by anyone who could walk, ride a horse or bring a wagon with mules. Jonathan Cox even came with his younger brother, Andy and his mother and he even closed down the store for the day cause everyone would be there to help put up the barn anyway. All the women brought food and drink to keep the men going. The barn would be up before sundown. That evening everyone came back for the wing ding. Those that lived too far to go home and come back went home with different people to get cleaned up for the evening festivities. Many homes would be open for guests to stay over night that needed to.

The musicians arrived and would set up on a platform that would be built in the barn for them. Until that happened they also pitched in to help raise the barn. One of the musicians was a black man named Jody Wilcox who had been working on the railroad with Mary's father, Ed Maney. Ed told Charles about Jody and what a good banjo player he was. Charles had asked Ed to invite Jody to come play with the band. Everyone was excited about hearing him play.

"Jody, does that little girl of yours show any interest in the music?" Ed asked him as he tuned his banjo.

"She saw some buck dancing last fall at a barn raising and she fancies her feet have wings now," Jody chuckled. He turned to look at his 13-year-old daughter, Tiara. She intently watched the other children.

Lila Ann and Mary were watching everything come together on one of the large bails of hay that had been placed around the barn for people to sit on. Joe Henry came into the barn and noticed them and decided to join them. Mary smiled up at him through her dark eyelashes.

"Are you going to dance with me tonight, Mary?" asked Joe Henry as he sat down next to her.

"If you'll show me how I will," Mary replied.

"Gosh, I thought you'd show me," Joe Henry chuckled.

"Maybe we can just teach each other," Mary laughed.

"What do you think about that, cousin?" Joe Henry had noticed something across the room had caught Lila Ann's attention. Joe Henry followed her stare with his eyes and focused in at the band platform. Mary looked at the cousins and looked to see what they were looking at.

"That man sure is black!" Joe Henry broke the silence.

"I've never seen someone with skin that dark," Lila Ann said. And about that time Lila Ann's eyes and Tiara's eyes met.

"That must be his relative because her skin is almost as dark as his!" Lila Ann commented.

"That is Jody Wilcox and he works with my Daddy, "Mary replied, "and that little girl is his daughter, Tiara. Mom said that Jody was going to bring her. I've not met her before but Mr. Wilcox talks about her when he comes to our house."

"Why is his skin so dark?" Joe Henry asked matter-a-factly.

"Haven't you ever seen a black man before?" Mary was surprised, "They are known as Negroes and they come from Charleston, South Carolina."

"How did their skin get so dark?" Lila Ann asked and continued, "Did they stay in the sun too long?"

"No, they are a race of people like me and you," Mary chuckled, "Their ancestors came from a country called Africa."

"How did you know all that, Miss Mary?" Joe Henry asked.

"Cause I had the same questions you did when I first saw Mr. Wilcox. And daddy explained to me that their family members had been slaves brought over from Africa. Mr. Wilcox's granddaddy had been a freed slave, when the Civil War was over," Mary explained.

"Since you know her daddy, why don't you go over and ask her to come over here and sit with us?" Lila Ann said as she turned to look at Mary.

"Let's all go over there," Joe Henry interrupted, "I want to see that musical instrument he is going to play. I've never seen anything like that before!"

All three children jumped down and headed toward the platform. They never noticed how quiet things had gotten and how others were watching there journey across the barn to the stranger that had come to play and his strange new instrument.

"Hello, Mr. Wilcox," Mary said as they got closer to the platform. "Is that the instrument you were telling me about?"

"Oh hello Mary," Jody Wilcox turned to smile at the children, "Yes, this is called a banjar. I made this instrument. The first one of these I ever saw was a washtub with a broom stick attached to it and strings pulled down from the top of the stick to the tub."

"I'd sure like to have seen you hold that in your lap and try to play it!" Ed Maney chuckled.

"Yeah, back then I was about the size of that stick and I stood next to my grandfather and watched him pluck the stings. It sure made strange sounds but my grandfather said we were not allowed to play our drums that were brought over from Africa so we made new instruments," Jody said as his fingers began to move on the strings of the banjo and the most delightful sounds drifted across the barn.

"My father made a banjar out of a calabash gourd that was cut off and attached to a wooden neck. A hole was cut in the gourd and covered with ground hog hide or goatskin. He used horsehair for the strings. I made this one I'm playing out of wood and goatskin and horsehair." When Jody finished his brief history of the banjo or banjar as he called it, his fingers began to fly on the horsehair strings.

Ed picked up his guitar and joined in and this set off a chain reaction with the other musicians, soon the fiddle played by Fate and a French Harp joined in. The children just stood there absolutely mesmerized by this new kind of instrument. They watched in amazement as Jody's hands moved so swiftly over the strings and soon several people were out dancing to the swift-moving music.

That is when Jody's daughter, Tiara caught Lila Ann's eye again. Tiara had slowly slipped out a short distance from the platform. She just couldn't resist the beat of the music like many of the dancers clogging on the hard barn floor where she was dancing. The children circled around her and started clapping. This brought a big smile to Tiara's face.

Soon the barn began to fill with people, the band playing brought everyone in and Lockie came in with Charles. Charles carried Aaron and Lockie lead Jimmy by the hand. Everyone started to applaud for the young couple. Charles handed the baby to his wife and got up on the platform to say something to his friends and family. The band stopped to give Charles audience.

"Friends and family, I wanted to thank each and every one of you for all the help you have given to me and Lockie and our young'uns in getting the barn raised today. My new house is finished, thanks to you, Jonathan Cox. And Mrs. Amanda Cox, we're all so glad to have you here tonight after suffering the loss of your husband and a bad bout with the flu. We are honored that you were able to come."

Everyone applauded again until Charles raised his arms to say, "Now, my Lockie has practiced singing her ballads all day so I'm going to get her up here to sing that long-winded one first while everyone isn't too tired to hear it. And then the band will play some dancing music after she is finished."

Everyone applauded again as Lockie got on the platform and Charles took the two boys. As Lockie prepared to sing, Mary asked Lila Ann, "Is that the song about 'Little Mathey Groves' that he is talking about?"

"Yes. It is an old English ballad or kind of a love song that my Granny taught to Mommy. Mommy has been singing since she was a young girl. She told me once that when she was my age her schoolteacher's sister came to visit from up north. The schoolteacher's sister was some kind of Music Professor. She heard Mommy singing one of her ballads in the school yard one day and was asking Mommy all about it. She told Mommy she knew about those ballads and that they came from England and some from Ireland and Scotland. She said that the ballads were really old, like over two hundred years old! She said she wanted to collect the ballads, which means write them down. She said she knew people in England who would love to know about them too."

"Did she write them down?" Mary asked.

"No, she must have got busy doing something else," Lila Ann said.

During the speech by Charles, Tiara had gone back to the platform to sit down. Without meaning to, Charles had broken the spell of her first encounter with these mountain children. She knew that would change. When Tiara Wilcox looked into Lila Ann's eyes the first time, she knew she'd have a new friend.

About that time Lockie cleared her throat, ready to begin a very long ballad. Many mountain ballads were performed without music as this one would be. And she began...

LITTLE MATHEY GROVES

Oh holiday, Oh holyday, the first day of the year.
Little Mathey Groves to church did go,
Some holy words to hear, hear,
Some holy words to hear.

He spied some women dressed in black as they came into
view. Lord Daniel's wife was gaily clad,
The flower of the few, few,
The flower of the few.

She stepp'd up to little Mathey Groves,
Her eyes cast on the ground,
Said please, oh please come with me stay,
As you pass through this town, town,
As you pass through this town.

Oh please, oh please, come with me stay,
I 'II hide thee out of sight.
I 'II pleasure you beyond compare
And sleep with you all night, night,
I 'II sleep with you all night.

I cannot stay, I dare not stay,
I fear t 'will cost my life.

Cause I can tell by your finger rings,
That you're Lord Daniel's wife, wife,
That you're Lord Daniel's wife.

Lord Daniel's in some distant land.
He's left me for to roam.
He's taken all his merry men
And I am quite alone, lone,
And I am quite alone.

Her little footy page was standing nearby
Was hearing every word was said.
He said before the sun goes down,
Lord Daniel will know what's said, said,
Lord Daniel will know what's said.

He ran along the King's Highway.
He swam against the tide.
And before the sun went down
He's standing by Daniel's side, side,
He's standing by Daniel's side.

What news, what news Lord Daniel cried
What news do you bring to me?
My tenants wronged?
My castle burned?
My wife with a baby, by, my wife with a baby?

No harm has come to your house or lands
While you have been away.
But little Mathey Groves is hugg'n and a kiss'n on your fair
lady, gay, gay,
On your fair lady gay.

If what you say is not the truth as I take it to be
I'll build a scaffold tower so high and hang'd you will be,
be,
And hang'd you will be.

If what I say is not the truth and false as false can be
You need not build a scaffold tower
Just hang me from a tree, tree,
Just hang me from a tree.

Lord Daniel called his merry men
And bid with them with him go
But warned them not to speak a word
And not a horn to blow, blow,
And not a horn to blow.

But riding with his merry men was one who'd wish no ill.
He put his bugle to his mouth
And he blew it loud and shrill, shrill,
And he blew it loud and shrill.

What is this? Cried little Mathey Groves as he sat up in
bed.
I fear it is your husband's men
And I will soon be dead, dead,
And I will soon be dead.

Oh lay back down little Mathey Groves
And keep by back for cold
T' is nothing but my father's men calling their sheep to
fold, fold, Calling their sheep to fold.

So little Mathey Groves, he laid back down
And soon fell off to sleep.
When he woke up, Lord Daniel was standing at his bed
feet, feet, Was standing at his bed feet.

Saying how do you like my snow-white pillow?
How do you like my sheet?
Saying how do you like my pretty little woman
That's lay'n in your arms asleep, sleep,
That's a lay'n in your arms asleep?

Get up, get up Lord Daniel cried
And put on your clothes.
In England, it shall never be said that I killed a naked
man, man, That I killed a naked man.

I won't get up, I can't get up.
I fear t 'will cost my life
Cause you have got two bitter swords
And I ain't got a knife, knife,
And I ain't got a knife.

I know I've got two bitter swords,
They cost me deep in purse.
I '11 give to you the best of these
And I will keep the worst, worst,
And I will keep the worst.

The first swing that little Mathey made,
It hurt Lord Daniel sore.
The next swing that Lord Daniel made
Little Mathey hit the floor, floor,

Little Mathey hit the floor.

Get up, get up, my pretty little wife
And come sit on my knee.
And tell me which you liked the best
Little Mathey Groves or me, me,
Little Mathey Groves or me?

She looked up in Lord Daniel's face
And saw his jutting chin.
Said, I wouldn't trade Little Mathey Groves
For you or all your kin, kin,
For you or all your kin.

He took her by her lily white hand
And led her across the hall.
He pulled out his sword and cut off her head
And kicked it against the wall, wall,
And kicked against the wall.

Go dig a grave both wide and deep
To bury these two in.
Just kick little Mathey Groves over the side
But lower my sweet wife in, in,
Yes, lower my sweet wife.

When Lockie had finished her ballad everyone applauded and people started hollering out other ballads for her to sing.

She replied, "That took all my wind to sing let's let the band play and I'll come back later and sing another in a little while.

With Lockie finished and the music continuing on for people to dance, Lila Ann remembered Tiara and the wonderful way she moved to the fast music. Her feet looked like they had wings as they moved in time to the swift beat of her Daddy's banjo.

"You are a very good dancer," Lila Ann said after walking over to where Tiara sat and it startled Tiara so much so she jumped.

All the children that were around them began to giggle including Tiara. Mary had joined Lila Ann and spoke too, "Your Daddy has talked a lot about you. Where did you learn to dance like that?"

"Oh I watched some of the men buck dance at the places my Pap goes to play music. I love the music and I just can't be still whilst it's a play'n! So I started to get up and dance too," Tiara replied.

"My name is Tiara," she said with a big smile. She had hoped all evening that she could make some new friends.

"Hello, my name is Lila Ann and this is Mary, her daddy works with yours. And this is my cousins, Joe Henry and Nathan."

Mary asked, "Are you and your Daddy going to live around here?"

"Yes, whilst he is working on the railroad but we '11 go home to Charleston when he is finished cause that is where all my family lives," Tiara explained.

"Come on over and sit with us," Lila Ann invited.

"Tiara, do you think your Daddy would teach me to play that banjar?" Joe Henry asked as they turned to walk back to the bale of hay.

"Oh, yes," Tiara smiled at Joe Henry, "he had several students back home that he was teaching. He can even help you make your own banjar."

"Wow! I can hardly wait! You girls go on. I'm going back and watch him play," Joe Henry said as he turned around.

The barn dance went on until the wee hours of the morning. The children, of course, were put to bed before the dance ended with some falling asleep before they were taken out of the barn. Lila Ann, Anna Jane and Jimmy were curled up snuggly in their large feather bed. Lila Ann drifted off to sleep dreaming of the new house, her new bedroom and the new friend she had made. Her last thoughts as she drifted off to sleep was- "It's so good to be home in my mountains."

CHAPTER 14
THE FLOOD

"I'm just a poor wayfaring stranger, traveling through this world of woe. But there's no sickness, no toil or danger in that bright world to which I go. I'm goin' there to see my father. I'm goin' there no more to roam. I'm just a goin' over Jordan. I'm just a goin' over home," Lockie sang as she milked her cow in her new barn.

She stopped squirting the cow's milk into the wooden pail when she thought she heard an echo just outside the barn. She could hear the words, "over home" coming back at her from outside. It did not sound like her voice, but it was definitely singing. She was so curious she got up to go look and see what or who it was or if she was just hearing things.

When she got to the barn door all she saw was Anna Jane, Jimmy, and baby Aaron. They were all sitting on a blanket she had placed on the ground for them to play on while she milked the cow. Lockie loved to sing for the cow because it calmed her down and she didn't kick the milk bucket over.

Lockie decided to continue her song right there at the barn door. She softened her voice so she wouldn't startle the children who hadn't yet seen her standing there. "I know dark clouds will gather around me. I know my way is rough and steep. Yet beauteous fields lie just before me, where God's redeemed their vigils keep. I'm goin' there to see my mother. She said she'd meet me when I come. I'm just a goin' over Jordan. I'm just goin' over home."

About halfway through her first sentence in the song, Anna Jane started singing with her. She managed to keep just behind Lockie's words repeating what Lockie sang one beat behind her. And what was interesting was Anna Jane was very good. Aaron loved it because he clapped his plump little hands when Anna Jane sang as if trying to keep the beat to the music too. The children still hadn't noticed their mother standing there so she continued with the third verse.

"I will be free from every trial. My body will sleep in the churchyard. I'll drop the crown of self-denial and I'll enter in for my reward. I'm going there to see my Savior to sing His praise forevermore. I'm only goin' over Jordan.

I'm goin' over home, I'm only goin' over, over, over home," Lockie finished she listened to Anna Jane finish on her own exactly as her mother had.

"Well, my goodness, Anna Jane. You sound better than me!" Anna Jane's head jerked up in surprise as Lockie continued, "How long you been singing like that?"

"I don't know, Mommy," Anna Jane replied and seemed a little bit embarrassed. Singing had been so natural to Anna Jane; she didn't even realize or think about doing it. To Anna Jane it had always been her mother singing, she just liked to follow along. Anna Jane sure didn't know how to explain what just happened naturally like breathing.

"Joe Henry and I are going to ride horses up on the mountain and meet Mary near her cabin," Lila Ann walked up to save Anna Jane from any more explanations of why she was singing along with her mother. Lila Ann looked from her mother back to her sister and asked, "What is wrong?"

"Oh, nothing is wrong," Lockie smiled down at Anna Jane, "I was just telling Anna Jane what a beautiful voice she had when she was singing along with me." This comment surprised Anna Jane and pleased her deeply that her mother wasn't upset with her as she first suspected.

"Oh, Anna Jane has always sung along when you start singing and I always tell her to hush so I can hear you sing ever since I can remember," Lila Ann said matter-a-factly.

"Well, how come I have never heard Anna Jane singing?" Lockie asked.

"Probably because when you stop singing so does Anna Jane," Lila Ann shrugged her shoulders.

Lockie's eyes glistened with tears, "I had always hoped one of you would carry on the ballads!"

"I know all the ballads, Mommy," Anna Jane gushed, "sometimes I sing them for Jimmy if he wakes up scared at night." Lockie reached down and kissed both of Anna Jane's rosy cheeks and then enveloped her in her arms. She looked up at Lila Ann, "Say you're going riding with Joe Henry?"

"Yes'um," Lila Ann smiled.

"Anna Jane and I are going to be practicing some singing before the noon meal. Would you like to pack a lunch to take with you? Riding horses can make you hungry and I know Joe Henry will be." Lockie looked up at the sky, "If it looks like it might rain, you both high tail it home, okay?"

"Yes'um, I sure will," promised Lila Ann as she headed for the kitchen to get the left-over biscuits and fill them with butter and jelly.

Just as Lila Ann finished wrapping the biscuits and storing them in a small lard bucket she heard Joe Henry's horses ride into the front yard.

"Looking for Lila Ann?" Lockie asked Joe Henry as he rode up where Lockie and Anna Jane, also Jimmy and baby Aaron were sitting on a blanket.

"Yes, Ma'am," Joe Henry smiled.

"She is packing you all a lunch to take with you, to meet Mary Maney," Lockie also mentioned, "If it starts to rain, head home, please, Joe Henry," Lockie continued, "These mountains can become a dangerous place to ride horses in the rain.

"Yes, Ma'am," Joe Henry replied as Lila Ann appeared at the kitchen door with the lard bucket in hand. She walked over to Joe Henry to hand the lard bucket up to him which was a safe way to carry food in the mountains after the lard was used up and washed out.

"I got my horse saddled in the barn," Lila Ann turned toward the barn to fetch him. And Lockie commented as Lila Ann came out of the barn already mounted on the horse, "Summer storms can be full of lightning that can easily spook horses," Lockie said.

Joe Henry and Lila Ann rode off, side by side as Lila Ann called over her shoulder, "Don't worry, Mom, we will be okay."

Lockie went over to the blanket to pick up baby Aaron, "Come on, Anna Jane, get Jimmy's hand, let's go fix some lunch and then, you young'uns can take a nap. Your daddy will also be hungry when back from Uncle Fate's House."

Just as Charles came into the yard a huge clap of thunder struck behind the barn and his horse reared up in fright. "Whoa! Champ!" Charles pulled on the reins of his horse, jumping off of the horse onto the ground, still holding the reins so the horse couldn't run off.

Lockie appeared at the barn door looking at Charles holding the horse and talking to him while he rubbed the horse's nose to calm him down more. "Was that thunder I heard that spooked Champ?" Lockie asked.

"Yes, and my horse nearly threw me out of the saddle so I slung my foot over and jumped off the saddle and started rubbing his nose to calm him down." Charles started slowly walking him toward the barn

"I should have known those kids would have a storm, I thought about that when I heard the thunder, I told them to come home if it started to rain," Lockie said as she stepped outside to look up at the sky.

"Where were they going?" Charles asked as he headed toward the barn with Lockie trailing behind him.

"To visit with Mary Maney up at her cabin," Lockie followed her husband, talking to him as he led his horse toward the barn and as they got closer to the barn, it started raining harder. She continued moving faster with him and the horse picked up his steps too, "They told me if it looked like a storm, they would put the horses in the Maney's barn and stay with Mary and her mom in their cabin."

Charles went into the barn with the horse to feed him and prayed the lightning wouldn't spook the horses that Joe Henry and Lila Ann were on before they got to Mary's. "You know these animals are very sensitive to storms," He turned to Lockie and said, "Reach me an apple out of that basket, Champ loves them." As Charles put Champ in his stall and gave him the apple that Lockie got from the basket, he rubbed Champ's nose again as Champ was chomping on the apple, Lockie asked, "Are you sure the kids will be okay? Tomorrow when it stops raining, can you go check on them?" Charles smiled, "Sure."

"I've got some lunch ready. Lila Ann made a lunch for herself and Joe Henry. And I stuck a few things in her bucket for Mary and her mom as well," Lockie said.

"I hope that thunder and lightning don't get to them until they get to Mary's cabin, and I pray, no rain either," Lockie went to the barn door to look out as the rain was falling harder, "And I hope this is over soon."

Charles came over to Lockie with his flannel shirt held over their heads to make a run for the kitchen door, as he said, "Don't worry, Lockie. Whatever happens we will pray about it before we go to sleep. Cause I have a feeling this storm will last all night." And they both ran for the kitchen door.

And the rain didn't fall on Joe Henry and Lila Ann until they got to Mary's barn to put their horses in it. "Wow! I could hear the rumbling behind us," Lila Ann said as she opened the barn door for their horses.

Mary was in the barn too. "I was wondering if you two would even come when I heard the distant rumbling.

Lila Ann jumped when she heard Mary's voice. Her eyes were just getting use to the darkness in the barn when Mary spoke and startled her. "I'm sorry, I frightened you, Lila Ann. I'd forgotten this barn can be so dark when you come in during daylight." Mary giggled.

"I guess we will end up here for the night," Lila Ann giggled too, "I brought us some lunch and also for you and your mom too.

"Well, you two may end up here for the night cause it sounds like it is going to be a big one," Mary peered out the barn door as it started to rain, " Mom can make us pallets on the floor and we can tell haint stories."

"That sounds like fun!" Joe Henry smiled. "But I'm hungry. Let's go in and eat before the rain gets harder. I'll come out during the night to check on the horses and see that they don't get spooked. It sounds like lightning is coming along too.!"

CHAPTER 15
THE FLOOD DESTROYS

The family at Lockie's new home was shaken awake when a landslide came from the mountain beside their home bringing rocks and a few large boulders done on the left side of the house with the boulders hitting the side of the front porch and breaking some of the porch spindles in the process.

Aaron sounded his alarm by starting a loud whaling cry that brought everyone out of bed all ending up next to Aaron's crib as if his whaling shook the house. Charles diverted from the crib though, he knew the shaking of the house was outside the house.

Lockie looked around for Charles and saw him heading toward the front door, so she followed him picking up the crying baby first and handing him to Anna Jane. "Charles what on earth shook this house like that?" Lockie asked as she trailed behind him. She saw her answer when she caught up to Charles standing in front of what was left of their front porch. And it was still raining as it had all night soaking the ground until any more rain would have trouble finding other places to go. Lockie gently slide her arm under Charles's arm and gently squeezed it.

The wind was blowing against the couple and Lockie began to feel a chill run across her body, "Come back into the house, Lockie, you don't need to catch a cold from this sharp wind," Charles said as he put his arm around Lockie and pushed her back into the house. Charles was worrying about his other daughter and his nephew somewhere higher up on the mountain in a small cabin with their Cherokee friend as this storm raged on.

"I'm thinking about Lila Ann and Joe Henry, they are higher up on the mountain than we are, but slides will be happening in those higher places, the more this ground gets soaked," Charles said as he felt tiny fingers wrapping around one of his legs. "Jimmy, you, okay?" Charles asks as he reached down to pick little Jimmy up on his strong shoulders. Charles continued, "And I'm worried about Fate and Ora's house, it is much older than ours even this rough wind could do a lot of damage to that house. And John Laboree was a young man when he built that house, and he is almost 90 years old."

"But I can't go anywhere in this rain and wind, hopefully, it will lighten up some or STOP!" Charles looked outside as if he were talking to GOD. In the meantime, Lockie decided to fix some breakfast, so she set out to the kitchen to build a fire in her cookstove. It would take her mind off this storm, and hopefully everyone else's, "I'm going to fix some breakfast, any requests?" Lockie asked as she banked the fire and checked each eye of the stove to settle the burning pieces of wood to even out the fire.

"You put some coffee on?" Charles was the first one to appear in the kitchen. Lockie looked up and replied, "First thing I put on." Charles found a cup and waited for the coffee to finish perking.

"What are the children doing? They are awfully quiet, "Lockie said as she poured Charles's coffee in the cup he was holding. Charles reached over and kissed her forehead and said, "They are watching the storm from the front window."

Suddenly there was some commotion at the front door, and a rain-soaked Fate appeared at the kitchen door with children all around him dripping wet too and the last one adult to appear was Lockie's sister, Ora Laboree. She was soaked to the skin and very pregnant. Fate explained, "We didn't know where to head when a big tree fell on our house, and it started raining in our living room. Willie is at the house stacking up the living room furniture in one of the bedrooms so something might be saved, but we may go home to find the whole house gone. I see you have a landslide that hit your front porch."

Charles brought a chair over for Ora to set down and he stepped in the living room to fetch Lockie's coverlet to place around Ora until she could shed her wet clothes. Lockie came from behind Charles to hand Ora and Fate each a cup of steaming coffee. Charles ask Fate, "How did you get here?"

"We brought the Surrey with the two horses, but we lost the top of the Surrey to that whipping wind. So, I just pulled it off and threw it on the ground and we kept coming. Maybe we can fix it later. I put the horses in your barn and got some hay out for our horses and yours too. They were not too jumpy yet. What will happen if this rain keeps going another day?" Fate asked.

Charles walked over and rubbed Fate's shoulder, "I truly do not know, Fate. We will just have to take one day at a time. And tonight, we will do some serious praying, this is one thing only GOD can handle. I do know that both good and bad events work for good for GOD's plan for each person's life. Did you ever read the story of Joseph at the last part of Genesis? We could read part of that story tonight with the children."

"Is that the story where his brothers were jealous of him, and they sold him into slavery, and he was 17 years old? And he ends up being the second in command only to Pharaoh? Just about the time there was a 7-year famine in the mid-eastern countries?" Fate asked.

Nathan came in the front door with his brother Willie right behind, both boys were soaked, "Is Joe Henry here?" Willie asked looking around the living room. "I thought he and Lila Ann would be here." Anna Jane came over to Nathan and placed a towel around Nathan's shoulders to help him dry off some. She then gave Willie a towel because she couldn't reach his shoulders. She just looked up at Willie and said, "I guess they got rained in at Mary Maney's cabin, because that was where they were headed when it started to rain yesterday."

"Anna Jane, go upstairs and get Aunt Ora my robe so she can get those wet clothes off and get Fate some of Charles's clothes to replace his wet ones. And Nathan, you and Willie get over here behind the cookstove and your clothes will dry quickly. And I will finish breakfast and we will all sit down and eat. Willie and Nathan, here is each of you a cup of coffee," Lockie said as she handed each boy a cup.

A couple of miles away and a little higher in elevation, Lila Ann, Joe Henry, and Mary were sprawled out on the pallets in the floor around the fireplace of Mary's cabin. Mary's mom, Louise was up and cooking breakfast for Mary and her friends, when Ed, Mary's dad came in and stopped to look at the pallets with children on the floor in front of him, something he was not expecting, "My goodness, did Joe Henry and Lila Ann get caught out in this storm?" Ed noted as he started tiptoeing across the floor toward Louise.

"Well, sort of. The cousins were coming up to go riding and they came to see Mary and invite her along. They had no idea we were going to have this awful rain, no one did. It didn't start raining until after they got here on horseback. Mary was out getting her horse out to ride anyway, I'm sure glad they didn't have time to leave," Louise said, "And I figured if it got bad, you'd be called to help. Is it bad with the trains?"

"Yes, and it is only going to get worse if it continues all day again today. I thought I'd come home, get something to eat and check on my girls, and make sure you don't need anything. But I do have to go back, they have called everyone that can come back to work," Ed continued, "The town of Marshall is already got the French Broad River covering over the train tracks. And the houses on Main Street there are calling for the people to head for higher ground and leave their homes."

Smelling food cooking, the cousins and Mary began to wake up. And outside the rain continued that Sunday morning no one in the mountains would be going to church many towns had no churches to go to. It was July 16, 1916. And the rain stopped falling

CHAPTER 16
THE ARRIVAL OF AUGUSTUS BROWN

The two cyclones came together over the Western North Carolina Mountains at the same time was not predicted to happen as it was barely noticed by the Weather Bureau in Washington on July 12th, 1916. They only gave some indication that there was a disturbance in the extreme Eastern Caribbean Sea. Yet there was a tropical cyclone coming along the east coast from Charleston, S.C. on the 14th of July that turned northwestward toward the mountains and another tropical hurricane coming from the Gulf Coast of Alabama and this one was accompanied by high winds, reaching a maximum of 107 miles per hour. At Alta Pass, in Mitchell County where the rainfall was the heaviest, 22.22 inches of rain fell in the 24 hours proceeding 2 pm on the fateful Sunday, July 16th, 1916. At Old Fort, at the foot of the Blue Ridge, the Old Fort Sentinel stated, rivulets became streams, streams became creeks, creeks became rivers, and graphic phrase, "rivers became frightful." Asheville and Biltmore were flooded! The cry went out around and the water is up to the ceiling in the train depot.

At the Maney cabin above Marshall, N.C., Ed Maney gobbled down his breakfast. He was a Southern Railroad worker, and he knew from previous experiences that floods could destroy railroads and people would be stranded and passengers endangered, and people needed to be told about the damage that would happen to their homes if some didn't already know. "Joe Henry and Lila Ann, you two stay here, you have no idea how bad it is down this mountain, and you will be safer up here for now. If I hear anything about your family, I will get a message to you. And if I get an opportunity, I will check on them and let them know you two are okay as well."

At 4 o'clock Sunday morning flood torrents had burst without warning into the village of Biltmore; the rising waves drove the people to the hills for miles along the Swannanoa and French Broad Rivers, and houses were tossed in the waves like eggshells and lashed in pieces against the concrete bridges. Several people lost their lives. Two sisters who were nurses and who were graduates of the Clarence Baker Memorial Hospital, lost their lives.

Near the Tennessee border at the Ireland house Lockie and her sister, Ora, had their families at Lockie's new house all but the cousins, Lila Ann and Joe Henry who had gone toward Marshall to go horseback riding near their Cherokee friend's cabin on the mountain above the town of Marshall that sits right on the French Broad River. It was not raining when they first left Lila Ann's home to head up the mountain. And Rose, Ora's oldest child, was now married and living in Mars Hill near the small college where her husband was working.

"Have you heard anything from Rose and Tom before this awful rain started?" Lockie asked her sister while they were planning sleeping arrangements for the two large families. "I saw them a couple of days before the deluge hit. Tom was taking the Grandfather to his other son's, Claude, who lives in the Piedmont close to Morganton. A place called Hickory, N.C." Ora replied, "They were going to pick the Grandfather up later after he collects some of his things from Claude's place to bring back up here."

"Well, I hope they were able to avoid coming through a flooded Asheville," Lockie said, "We need to go check on the damage to your house. I can't imagine your rained out living room. At least Willie, bless his heart, had enough sense to move your living room furniture somewhere else," Lockie continued, "And from a look at the landslide next to this house is needed to make sure the mountain won't cave in more."

On Monday morning Ed Maney decided to go see Lila Ann and Joe Henry's family, see how each had survived after the rain had ended. He first came upon the Laboree place and inspected the damaged house. The big tree was still in place across the living room. Ed assumed the family had all gone to the Ireland house as he rode up on his horse, he noticed the damaged front porch and saw Fate and Charles walking around the back of the house. "Hello, Ed," Fate said, and Charles looked up to wave at Ed. "Are you checking out the damages up here?" Fate asked.

"I told Lila Ann and Joe Henry I'd come by and let you both know they are fine. Louise made them pallets on the floor in front of the fireplace. We have enjoyed their company. They have had fun telling haint stories to each other," Ed said.

"Tell us, did Marshall survive the flood at all?" Fate asked. "Well, most of Marshall didn't," Ed said and hung his head down, "First reports from Marshall, stated that practically nothing was left standing but the courthouse and the jail. Fifty-three houses were said to have been carried away and three lives lost. Marshall's Main Street is the only street there is, and its level is probably fifteen feet above normal river tide. The railroad runs close to the French Broad River and Main Street is about 100 feet from the river. Marshall was forced to call for outside aid. They were cut off from the outside world, except for dirt roads, which were in bad condition. It may take a while for some aid to get to them. Most of the people that lived in those houses that got washed away lost everything and had no clothes, food, or even a blanket to keep them warm at nighttime." Ed continued, "There will be no trains for at least three weeks or more. And you should see the train tracks that I've been checking out some iron rails can't even be reused because they are bent by the force of the water and some tracks are hanging in mid-air where the water washed away the ground underneath them, tunnels have cave-ins and need to be cleaned out and the debris is so piled up, that it will take an army to get it removed."

"Are you headed back to Marshall, Ed?" Charles asked, "What can we do to help? We will be planning the fixing of our houses, but they aren't too damaged and luckily the rain didn't cause us too much loss, my crops of corn and wheat are gone. We had a surplus last year but with a lot of families with such need, we want to help them. We can try to offer some shelter for those who have none, of course. And we could put some families up in the Baptist Church and some of the other church buildings in the different communities."

"The first and most important is to find the people that have survived, and see to their immediate needs," Ed said, "I heard a group of five automobiles, all Fords were headed from Weaverville to Marshall to get to the marooned with some food and blankets and dry clothes. One of the supervisors from the Southern Railway is also sending a large car full of provisions for a stranded train filled with passengers stranded at Nocona which is four miles below Marshall. Some of the passengers from that train came back with the four smaller automobiles about four of them in each auto to Asheville," Ed also mentioned, "We will need help from any able-bodied man or boy to start cleaning up the debris, Southern Railway will hire anyone who is willing to work. They will also provide food and comfortable sleeping quarters while they are employed with us. It will really help to get these trains running again as soon as possible. Please pass the word along to anyone who is interested. I will pick up the posters at the depot in Asheville which is where I am headed now."

"We sure will," Fate said, "I think Willie will be interested but I'll keep Nathan here he can help us get these houses livable again. Then Charles and I will gladly help especially getting Marshall cleaned up again. We will also check on your girls and let them know about all this."

That night the two families gathered in the Ireland home to make sure everyone had a comfortable sleeping place. Lockie put baby Aaron in the left corner of the house in a tiny storage room so the noise of people wouldn't disturb his sleep. "I'm going to put Aaron to bed, I put his crib in the storage room next to our bedroom. It should be nice and quiet in there, so everyone can talk or read or do homework in the parlor and you won't have to whisper," Lockie said, "Ever since Friday night's house shacking by that landslide, he hasn't been sleeping good."

"Of course, Lockie, we will be going to bed early anyway, because we are all quite tired from all this mess. This has been the most exhausting thing I have ever had to go through in my life and if I just sit down, I will fall asleep just sitting," Ora yawned.

Everyone did go to sleep early, it was 9 pm but in July the light still lingered. The ground did something that was so like the 2nd day of the deluge of rain, it started shacking and the earth sounded like a growling lion or mountain bear, then something hit the left side of the house again and brought everyone out of bed and up from their pallets in the living room floor around the fireplace. "What on earth is happening now?" Charles came growling out of his bedroom and a strong breeze hit him right in his face, but it wasn't coming from the front door, it came from the storage room that was next to his bedroom. The wind had blown the storage room door open with a wet oozing mud river running where the storage room use to be, and the mud river was headed toward the Laurel River which fed into the French Broad River.

Lockie awoke with a startled chill running over her, "Charles what is going on? I feel like someone just walked over my grave. I must have been having a bad dream or something," Lockie looked at Charles's terrified face and followed the glazed look to where his eyes were fixed, "Charles, the storage room is gone!" and Lockie fainted at Charles's feet.

Charles bent over to see if Lockie was okay, by the time Charles brought her out of the faint, everyone was crowded around the couple realizing that baby Aaron was gone somewhere on that muddy slide. Charles and Fate hit the back door to chase the new muddy river toward the only hill that the muddy river could go. In the meantime, Ora had a tearful sister realizing her baby would be in his crib hopefully still alive and screaming for his mommy. Willie had put his shoes and followed Fate and Charles in search of Aaron in his crib. Willie stopped to get a lantern and lit it before he followed the two men because it was getting dark.

Lockie ran back to her bedroom the find some shoes and put on a shirt and some pants so she could follow the men wherever that muddy river took them, "Ora find me another lantern and light it they will need more than one to search for my baby."

"I'll find two lanterns and get dressed too. I'll go with you. The more light, the better chance to see him," Ora headed for some pants and shirt too and some shoes." Each woman with a lit lantern headed out the back door.

The women finally saw their husbands up ahead with Willie holding the only lantern. They could see where the muddy river joined the Laurel River and water mixing with the muddy and started moving faster, moving toward the larger French Broad which looked bigger than ever. As they got closer to the joining rivers, Lockie yelled out to Charles, "Do you see or hear baby Aaron or his crib?"

Charles turned in surprise to see both women coming up behind him and Fate, "We can see the crib, it is caught on a tree limb, but the mattress and baby Aaron are nowhere in sight. Fate thinks the mattress is light and so is Aaron and we think they kept moving by the current. You must be careful, and I don't want either one of you to fall into this water, just walk over to that hill and look down on the French Broad River and see if you can see the mattress and the baby."

Lockie and Ora took their lanterns with them and headed to the hill that Charles was pointing too. Both holding the lanterns up high in order to see the French Broad below them. The current in the big river had slowed down somewhat since the water level was receding a lot with one day without rain. Lockie stood on her toes holding onto Ora's shoulder to try and get the lantern even higher, "I see him lying on that mattress slowly moving down the French Broad! He isn't moving though, oh Charles please go to him," Lockie started to cry.

Willie jumped into action, he headed for his aunt and his mother, "Mom, give me your lantern and I will follow the Laurel River to the French Broad, it isn't very far down to where the rivers join, I can move faster than Uncle Charles or Dad and the cold water won't bother me as much." Ora handed her son the lantern and Willie disappeared over the hill. Charles and Fate followed Willie at a slower pace, he might need their help to get to the mattress and the baby.

When Willie got to the edge of the French Broad River, he waded into the big river slowly so he would not overturn the mattress that the baby was on and Aaron moved a little, he was an exhausted baby after the rough ride down two rivers and he had fallen asleep. Willie gently pulled the mattress over to the side of the river, where he had left the lantern. The current wasn't too strong so he could manipulate the mattress, when he got it out of the water, he gently got a now loudly crying baby in his arms and looked up at his family and told them, "Aaron is fine, he was tired and cried himself to sleep when he got into a slower moving river, as you can hear he is alive!"

Lockie and Ora were both crying and Lockie raised her hand toward heaven and cried, "Thank You, LORD!" And they headed over to the hill as Willie and a still crying baby came up the river, "And thank you my sweet nephew, Willie, for catching my sweet baby," Lockie and Charles with baby Aaron wrapped their arms around the baby until he stopped crying. Willie, Ora, and Fate circled around and did a family hung too; they were all so thankful that the baby was alive.

It was an unusual storm with several months of labor to dig out from the mud and boulders to remake the roads and remove the debris of all the broken houses left behind. One unusual event was the Swannanoa River that changed its course in two places near Asheville. At the Cheeseborough residence on the river this strange occurrence took place and as a result in the latter case a quaint old spring house, built by the great grandfather of the present generation of the Cheesborough family and in use for one hundred years or more, was carried downstream and demolished.

Regular train service between Asheville and Black Mountain was instituted on July 24th, 1916. Southern Railroad really did this clean up with hundreds of workers also with the men in the communities that were so badly affected by this storm. These special workers were feed and housed in comfortable sleeping places and paid for their labor. Also, on this day when the railroad began running again a gentleman from England, Augustus Brown, was traveling to the Appalachian Mountains in interest of the ballads, old English, Irish, and Scottish Ballads. As with all things American, this influence blended with many other traditions in forming the very vibrant state of music throughout the region.

Along with Brown an assistant, Irene Hammond came along with her heavy typewriter during their travels to record the lyrics and Brown was an established music teacher and collector of traditional English songs and dances. Hammond's passion was dancing. She was a social worker helping at a settlement house and she developed a folk-dance club to engage the children with whom she was working.

When the couple finally arrived on Monday, July 24th, 1916, it was stifling hot in Knoxville, Tennessee, "Honestly, this weather is so humid that I can hardly breath!" Augustus remarked to Irene, "We must get a taxi over to the L & N Station and check our luggage. The conductor told me we could get rooms at the Blue Goose Hotel," Augustus said, "we will need to find some lunch, our train to Copper Hill doesn't leave until 4:34 pm."

Augustus and Irene walked into the Atkin Hotel, but the dining room wasn't open. So, they headed for the first restaurant they could find. Augustus commented over his shoulder to Irene, "Be careful what you eat, can't have you getting sick while we are in a slow-moving train." Irene giggled and said, "We can stop in a provision shop and buy some cheese and crackers."

The train was slow; indeed, they didn't arrive in Copper Hill until 10 pm. Augustus got his suitcase, but they couldn't find Irene's suitcase. "Well, we will go locate the Blue Goose and I can loan you some of my pajamas," Augustus chuckled, "You can go shopping tomorrow if they don't find your suitcase."

The next morning breakfast was around 6:00 am but the train wasn't ready to leave until 7:45 am and they never located Irene's suitcase. "I guess it was stolen. I'm glad I didn't have anything of value in it." And they arrived in Murphy, N.C. at 11:30 am.

The Campbells were waiting for them at the station. John and Olive Campbell later founded the John C. Campbell Folk School located in Brasstown, N.C. At the present they were living on the Biltmore Estate owned by George Vanderbilt who died in 1914, at the young age of 51 years. His wife still owns the Estate.

CHAPTER 17
BALLAD MUSIC COLLECTING IN THE MOUNTAINS

Mr. and Mrs. Campbell drove Augustus and Irene to their home on the Biltmore Estate, a large three-story house that sat up on a hill just above the Swannanoa River, "You are lucky your house is high up on this hill. Did the river below flood any?" Irene asked as they rounded the curve up to their house.

"Oh, yes, but it didn't get up to cover our road completely. But many of the farms that lie on lower ground got flooded. There is a pig farm over on the other side of our house that lost everything. The family that lived there just barely had time to get to our house with just their night clothes that they had on," Mrs. Campbell said, "We are trying to help them out as much as we can."

Augustus and Irene stayed at the Campbell's until Thursday, July 27th, Mr. Campbell's sister, Mrs. Ruth Carledge and her children were staying there also. It was a very large house and there was plenty of room. Irene spent Wednesday afternoon shopping for a new suitcase and things she'd need for it. On Wednesday night Augustus told Irene, "I'm ready to head for the mountains, White Rock in Madison County via Marshall." So, after a 7:00 am breakfast Mr. Campbell motored them to Weaverville where they and their luggage were transferred to a pair of horses and a Surry.

"This is the most frightening experience I have ever gone through," Augustus exclaimed, "There is not a vestige of a real road until you get to Marshall, nothing but deep mud, sometimes nearly up to the axles, or huge stones and boulders. Marshall is a horrible place, and it smells very badly after the devastating flood it suffered. I hope we get to Dr. Packhard's at White Rock soon. The smell along with this stifling heat are almost unbearable."

"Irene, do you know what the word 'Ballad' means?" Augustus asked as they were walking beside the Surry that Mr. Campbell was driving. Irene looked up at Augustus and giggled, "Is this a trick question?"

Augustus began to explain, remembering that Irene's passion was the dance, "A Ballad is a form of verse, often a narrative set to music. Ballads derive from the medieval French chanson Balladee or Ballade, which were originally 'dance songs'. Ballads were particularly characteristic of the popular poetry and songs of Britain and Ireland from the Late Middle Ages until the 19th century."

They were supposed to stay at a Dr. Packhard's house in White Rock in Madison County. They eventually got there, Augustus pulled out his pocket watch to look at the time, "It is 6 p.m. and that took pretty well eleven hours over thirteen miles to accomplish." Augustus was not disappointed though; it was a small house but very comfortable.

They stayed at White Rock for three days, when they left, they knew they would be back because they didn't catch some of the people at home. Augustus was pleased with what they did accomplish during their first two days of collecting, "We now have nine excellent songs as a result of our first days of collecting."

The next place they planned to go was Allanstand also in Madison County. There they met a mother of soon to be ten children by the name of Mrs. Mary Sands. She came to the Presbyterian Mission in Allanstand where they stayed for six days with the singers coming to them to sing the Ballads or Love Songs as they called them. "Augustus, there is a lady here named Lockie Ireland. She would like to sing you some tunes her mother and her grandmother taught her. She lives near Marshall, and they heard from Mary Sands about you," Irene said and brought Mrs. Ireland over to meet Augustus, "And this little girl is her daughter, Anna Jane, she sings too."

"Well, come in ladies what is the name of the tune you want to sing for me?" Augustus asked. Lockie cleared her throat and said, "You want ballads? My grandmother called them Love Songs" Lockie replied, "My favorite one is a long one and is very old, I think it came from England. And I sing it without music," Lockie said, "It is called 'Little Mathey Groves'," and Lockie began to sing. After about one-half hour she finished, and Anna Jane sang along but one beat behind her. Lockie patted Anna Jane's head. Augustus smiled and turned to study the mother and daughter singers, and said, "You both have an unusual way of singing together."

Lockie smiled looking down at Anna Jane she said, "Well, I can explain that. You see, Mr. Brown, I just found out Anna Jane could sing. She would sing along with me while I was singing, one of my favorite places to sing is while I do my house chores especially when I milk the cow. It helps to keep the cow calm and she doesn't kick the milk bucket over, in fact that's what I was doing when I discovered her singing with me. I heard someone finish up the Love song right behind me, so I looked outside, and I continued to sing to see who it was and that is when I discovered her talent, she has a beautiful voice. I was so surprised and pleased! We just must practice some so we can stop and start at the same time.

"That is an unusual story, do you ever perform for people?" Augustus asked, "and do you have any more songs you can share?" Lockie said, "Absolutely, I can think of 10 more and I'm sure I can come back when I have time to remember the others, will you be here another day?

"We will be here for several days, Lockie, do you know where White Rock is located or Alleghany?" Augustus asked, "That is the next two places we will be collecting, and we will be staying at Dr. Packhard's house in White Rock." Lockie smiled down at Anna Jane, "We can probably catch up with you." Lockie and Anna Jane started walking toward the door.

Irene came in after the Irelands left, "They were sweet, I hope they do come back. They both are very good singers. Did she talk about their house getting damaged by a mudslide and her baby boy being washed into the French Broad River? Her nephew saved the baby too." Irene said.

"And my goodness, both those ladies were special! That was the first child singer I think we have had! And didn't Mrs. Sands prove to be a prize folk singer? The six songs she sang for us was first rate!" Augustus exclaimed, "With all those children she must love to sing ballads to them all just to survive." Mrs. Sands gave them along with her friend Mrs. Gasnell gave them songs every day that they stayed in Allanstand. On Wednesday, Mr. Campbell went back to White Rock to bring Augustus his tune book and Irene her typewriter. They would soon have to find another man to transport them by the name of Tom Shelton driving his pair of mules. He would be there on Saturday, August 5th, 1916, to assist them back to Dr. Packhard's again.

Augustus was packing when Irene came to see if he was ready to go, "Didn't we get some wonderful tunes from Mrs. Sands and Mrs. Gasnell again? Those ladies are surely prize singers. It will be good to see the Packhards again. There small house is a very comfortable place to stay, and his wife is a marvelous cook." Augustus replied, "Are you ready to ride the 'jolt wagon' again?"

Sunday was spent at the Packhards, enjoying their meals, writing out tunes in the tune book and letters to family and friends. Augustus enjoyed a smoke on the verandah while doing more letters and then off to bed.

Augustus and Irene decided to head to Alleghany, "The Postman, Clifford Shelton, said he would bring our luggage and your typewriter so we can have a nice walk to Alleghany. It will be a little hot, but I think the walk will do us good. Miss Bacon will kindly take you in for the night, Irene. And I will stay in the cabin in a cot bed, rather primitive quarters, I believe but okay." Augustus and Irene had spent six days at Alleghany collecting many tunes and doing a lot of walking in very hot sometimes rainy weather.

The next place they went in Madison County was Big Laurel and Rice Cove. They spent four days there collecting tunes. "We will head back to White Rock. We will get Mr. Wallen to take us to Marshall in his motor car," Augustus said to Irene, "Then we will head back to Asheville to the Biltmore Estate and the Campbell's house."

On Tuesday, August 22, 1916, Irene, Mrs. Carledge, and Mrs. Campbell went on an excursion to Mount Mitchell, which has the highest peak in all the Appalachian Mountains. Augustus stayed behind to write tunes in his tunes book. He also did some shopping before a tremendous thunderstorm burst over Asheville. It was about 2 p.m. when the storm hit. The ladies never got home from their excursion until 8 p.m. Augustus and Irene finished their packing along with Mr. Campbell who came with them to catch the train from Asheville to Hot Springs.

In Hot Springs they were in Madison County again. They stayed at the Dorland-Bell school, a Presbyterian Mission, now part of Warren Wilson College. Breakfast was at 7:00 a.m. "Irene," said Augustus, "Let us sally forth and cross this French Broad River. This ought to be an interesting adventure better than that wobbly foot bridge there is a punt with the aid of a wire manipulated by the ferryman, this looks like a bit of a perilous business to me. We will be visiting a Mrs. Jane Gentry." Mrs. Gentry held the record of the most tunes of any one person in the five states they collected. She gave them a total of 70 songs in several different trips to visit her.

After spending three days at Hot Springs this time, they do come back in September and spend six more days. They spend five more days at White Rock collecting tunes and then spend six days at Rocky Fork and Alleghany again spending three more days there collecting. "I am exhausted, Irene. Let's go back to Asheville for a few days' rest, do some shopping, and catch up my paperwork and write down my tunes that we have collected, and you can type up the words," Augustus said to Irene. So, they end up spending five days at the Campbells at the Biltmore Estate in Asheville.

This would finish their time in North Carolina until the Fall of 1918 when they found out that they could not go back to Hot Springs because of the WW1 German Internment Camp in the Mountain Park Hotel. The Mountain Park Hotel was owned by Col. Rumbough who negotiated with a contract with the War Department. They sent 2300 German soldiers to Hot Springs by train.

After traveling around the Northern part of America they went to New York to go back to England in December of 1916 on the S. S. Ryandam. Their return trip to collect ballads again was in April of 1917. They worked in Tennessee and Kentucky and in June of 1917 came back to Asheville, but not to collect tunes, Augustus needed to have some dental work done. This took almost two weeks to do.

Augustus and Irene prospected through Virginia and didn't get many tunes. They entered North Carolina again through Winston Salem and remembered a small town called Marion. Augustus had really liked Marion and made a note in his mind that he would return there some day. While in Marion they did do some collecting and stayed for nine days.

"Well, Irene, you are looking much better today," Augustus said as they both were rocking in rocking chairs on the front porch of their small hotel in Marion. This September in the mountains was a wet one, but today was the first sunny day they had since collecting in Marion. "Are you ready to head to the higher mountains on the train?" he asked Irene.

"We have both been pretty sick, off and on, this whole stay here in Marion," Irene said, "You have been the sickest that I have ever seen you be since our collecting began. How do you feel, weak?"

"Yes, and the wet, coolish weather hasn't helped. And our collecting here in Marion hasn't been too successful, to say the least, "Augustus replied, "I was talking to a gentleman in the corner drug store, and he suggested we go to Burnsville. We need to take the train up the mountain to Alta Pass then to Spruce Pine and Burnsville is the next town due west. He also suggested we check out the NuWray Inn located on the Town Square. He said it is a wonderful place to stay and they have an excellent kitchen with great food."

Irene and Augustus talked about their collecting of tunes while on the train that was taking them up higher in elevation than Marion, it was 3000 feet up to Alta Pass and shortly after they left there, they got stuck for one hour because of a break down of a freight train up ahead of them, so they arrived in Burnsville two hours late. "These mountains are absolutely beautiful!" Irene said, "the most amazing views I have ever seen anywhere that we have been in America."

Augustus was thinking about the collecting they had done since they got back to North Carolina, "We only took down about 200 tunes in seven weeks, Irene," he continued, "That is less than average both in quantity and quality, I hope Burnsville has better stuff for us.

Their first view of Burnsville was the interesting Town Square and right in the middle sat the huge white three-story house with four two-story brick columns supporting the front porch. Formally known as the Ray Hotel, in 1916 it was purchased by William Wray, Sr. and reopened as the NuWray Inn. It became well known for the family style home serving and seating and the home grown food it served.

And of course, Augustus and Irene were excited about staying there and their late arrival due to the freight train that got stalled in front of their passenger train causing their two-hour delay, all the good rooms were already taken but Mr. Wray promised to move them to better rooms the next night.

"The weather is a little colder at 3000 feet, don't you think, Irene?" Augustus said, "This Inn is a pretty, quiet and cozy little place, this county seat of Yancey County, North Carolina." He and Irene walked into the temporary rooms and were not too displeased with them. But they looked forward to better ones tomorrow.

Although Augustus got up feeling a bit 'seedy' with bad neuralgia in his right eye, they both hit the ground running and began first calling on Mrs. Cheseborough whom they had met two years ago at the Knoxville conference. She invited them to lunch at 12:30 tomorrow. After tea they moved upstairs to two very pleasant rooms. They then headed out Mitchell Branch to start their collecting.

After spending ten days collecting tunes in Burnsville even on Sunday the 22nd of September 1918, they decided to take Monday off to do their paperwork and rest which they usually did on Sunday. They were busy working in an extra room where Mr. Wray had built a fire in the fireplace. They had an unexpected guest who had come over from Madison County.

"Excuse me Mr. Brown but you have a guest who wants to help you with your tune collecting. Her name is Lockie Ireland and her daughter, Anna Jane, as well as Lockie's sister, Ora Mae Laboree," Mr. Wray said as he showed Lockie and Anna Jane and Ora into the room.

"Oh, yes, Mrs. Ireland and Anna Jane, but I don't believe I've met Mrs. Laboree. Come in, come in, ladies. Let me find you all a seat," Augustus said as Irene and he looked for chairs for them to set in. "Tell me Mrs. Laboree, do you sing and do you know some ballads too? Did you all come all the way from Madison County?"

"Yes, we brought Ora's Surry and horses and came over. I didn't get a chance to come back while you were collecting in Madison County. I did remember more ballads and Ora remembered some I didn't, and she wanted to meet you. We have been busy fixing our houses from the flood. A tree fell on Ora's house and took the roof off at the living room and my house which was new, lost part of the front porch from a mudslide than after the rain had stopped a larger mudslide from that same mountain side took out the back of my house where my baby son, Aaron was sleeping. He was washed out with the slide still in his crib. Ora's son, Willie saved him from the French Broad River." Lockie explained and continued, "then Ora, who was pregnant before the flood, had her baby daughter, and we were busy to say the least."

"We had to help more than usual because our husbands were helping to clean up the debris that was so awful everywhere the flood had been," Ora chimed into the conversation, "When I had the baby Lockie had to help deliver her. We named her Sina Elizabeth. She is a beautiful red-haired baby."

"I found out that you had come back to Burnsville and had been collecting here," Lockie said, "So, Ora's husband, Fate, fixed the Surry and I got Ora's oldest daughter, Rose to watch baby Sina as well as baby Aaron and the other little ones, we came here hoping we could catch you."

"Well, I'm glad you did!" Augustus smiled down at Anna Jane and asked, "Have you and your mom been practicing singing together?" as Anna Jane nodded yes, Augustus continued, "Let's get started, shall we?" And they spent that afternoon collecting ballads from both ladies. Augustus and Irene stayed in Burnsville the longest time they ever stayed in any town in the Appalachian Mountains.

The last day they stayed at the NuWray Inn in Burnsville was October 10th, 1918. They had stayed at the Inn for 30 days. According to Augustus as he and Irene talked, "This is the best place we have ever stayed in, and we think unless it suddenly pans out that we shall stay here until we go to Asheville to prepare to go home to England. We have collected 1625 tunes in the three years we have traveled in five mountain states."

END

ABOUT THE AUTHOR

GERALDINE GARDNER GIRARD

GERALDINE GARDNER was born in the Appalachian Mountains and it was her father who gave her the love of these mountains. Although she did not grow up in the mountains her parents moved north after her father came home from fighting in World War II. He liked working on cars and they moved to Detroit, Michigan and he worked for General Motors. While in college she was studying Drafting & Design she became interested in Journalism. She took several courses and worked in the college newspaper. After moving back to the mountains, she attended Mars Hill University to study teaching specializing in Elementary Education & Middle-Grade Education as well as Visual Art, she taught Visual Art in the Madison County Schools for 13 years. She was active in many writing workshops and joined the Writer's Workshop in Asheville, NC. She worked on weekends as a docent for the Thomas Wolfe House. And also acted in their Living History which was performed in the 80s. She was published in the Asheville Citizen-Times and in many local newspapers and in the Thomas Wolfe Review.

www.ingramcontent.com/pod-product-compliance
Lightning Source LLC
Chambersburg PA
CBHW022051050726

47591CB00002B/482